CW00968769

Brooke Carlisle had more than her fair
share of Carlisle pride. It had been pride
which had made her break off her
engagement to Ty Marshall when she
had found him in her stepmother's arms;
and it was pride, too, which made her
refuse to sell Oakley Manor . . .

*Books you will enjoy
by LEIGH MICHAELS*

CAPTURE A SHADOW

Shelby was a successful editor of romantic fiction. It wasn't until she met Mark Buchanan, however, that she discovered just how difficult romance in real life could be!

O'HARA'S LEGACY

Kate was excited about her legacy. Owning a bookstore was just the job she needed. Until Ross appeared on the scene, and suggested she didn't know the first thing about it . . .

BRITTANY'S CASTLE

Since the break-up of her marriage to Ryan Masters, Brittany had concentrated on her first love—her career in banking. But could it be a satisfactory substitute for love, especially now that Ryan was very much on the scene again?

CARLISLE PRIDE

BY
LEIGH MICHAELS

MILLS & BOON LIMITED
ETON HOUSE   18–24 PARADISE ROAD
RICHMOND   SURREY TW9 ISR

*All the characters in this book have no existence outside
the imagination of the Author, and have no relation
whatsoever to anyone bearing the same name or names.
They are not even distantly inspired by any individual
known or unknown to the Author, and all the incidents
are pure invention.*

*The text of this publication or any part thereof may
not be reproduced or transmitted in any form or by any
means, electronic or mechanical, including photocopying,
recording, storage in an information retrieval system, or
otherwise, without the written permission of the publisher.*

*This book is sold subject to the condition that is shall
not, by way of trade or otherwise, be lent, resold, hired
out or otherwise circulated without the prior consent of
the publisher in any form of binding or cover other than
that in which it is published and without a similar
condition including this condition being imposed on the
subsequent purchaser.*

*First published in Great Britain 1987
by Mills & Boon Limited*

© Leigh Michaels 1987

*Australian copyright 1987
Philippine copyright 1987
This edition 1987*

ISBN 0 263 75736 6

*Set in Monotype Times 10 on 10 pt.
01-0787-62689*

*Typeset in Great Britain by
Associated Publishing Services
Printed and bound in Great Britain by
Collins, Glasgow*

CHAPTER ONE

SPRING at Oakley Manor . . . Could there be another spot on earth where the sun shone quite so brightly, and the flowers had the same perfect clarity of colour? And the smells! Brooke inhaled deeply as she walked across the sloping back lawn. The sharp scent of jonquils, softened by the delicate fragrance of the first early bluebells and the rich smell of dew-wet ground tickled her nose as she walked slowly towards the back door.

'I suppose it's possible that I'm prejudiced,' she murmured, with a half-smile that poked fun at herself. 'But there's still nowhere that can beat Oakley in the spring.'

In another week, the hillside would be hazy with bluebells. A couple of weeks after that would come lilac, and then irises and peonies, and another gorgeous summer at Oakley would be on the way.

It would be the first summer without her father. Sadness clutched at her throat. Who would have guessed a year ago what sweeping changes twelve short months could bring to the Carlisles? And what of the coming year? What waited for them in the months ahead?

'Don't borrow trouble,' she told herself sternly. 'You've never been known for your talent in predicting the future anyway.'

A plump robin, looking for worms in the loose earth of a flower bed, cocked his head to one side and watched her warily. Then, apparently deciding that she was harmless, he resumed his search for breakfast.

'Is that a message?' Brooke asked him quietly. 'Are you telling me I'd better get out into the world and scramble to put food on the table, too?' She sighed, looked back across the hillside blanketed in yellow, and opened the kitchen door.

At the breakfast bar, a child sat on a high stool, a bowl of cereal in front on her, stirring aimlessly. Her lower lip was thrust defiantly out, and as Brooke came in, the child gave a violent push at the book-bag that lay beside her bowl. It slid off the counter, taking a glass full of orange juice with it.

'Now see what you've done!' The teenage girl on the other side of the bar had jumped back, avoiding the worst of the splash, but a few drops had hit her brown tunic. 'I'll have to change, and this is the last clean uniform I have,' she complained. 'You little——'

'It was your orange juice,' the child returned. 'You shouldn't have left it there!'

The teenager wheeled around. 'Brooke, you should have seen it,' she appealed. 'Tara the Terrible did it on purpose!'

'Did not,' the child said calmly. She started stirring her cereal again.

'I did see it, Emily.' Brooke folded her arms, leaned against the counter, and looked directly and unblinkingly at the child. 'What about it, Tara?'

The little girl looked up. 'It was her orange jiuce,' she said. 'Emmy left it in my way, so it spilled.'

Brooke sighed. Another normal day at Oakley Manor, she thought. Not even eight o'clock, and Emily and Tara were already at it. Why, she wondered, had fate chosen to saddle her with not one but two younger sisters! They fought each other continually, but if anyone outside the family made a critical comment, they defended each other like wildcats.

'But you pushed it off, Tara,' Brooke said firmly. 'It doesn't matter whether you did it on purpose, you still get the honour of cleaning up the mess. Wet a cloth and wipe up the floor. Now!'

Tara sniffed once, and then climbed down from her stool.

'Would you look at this!' the teenager muttered, trying to brush drops of orange juice off her tunic.

Brooke reached for a towel and dampened a corner of it. 'This should take care of it,' she said, as she dubbed at the spots. 'What's the matter with Tara?'

Emily sniffed, with all the assurance of seventeen years old. 'She doesn't want to go to school. She thinks that since I graduated last week, she shouldn't have to go any more, either.'

'It's only fair,' muttered Tara. 'Why should she get out two weeks early?'

'The seniors always do. And there's just one problem with your logic,' Brooke told her. 'There's a bit of difference between a young lady who's in third grade and one who just finished high school.'

Tara thrust out her bottom lip. 'It isn't fair that she gets a longer vacation.'

'Some vacation!' snorted Emily. 'Frying hamburgers at the Burger Barn!'

'Speaking of which,' Brooke asked, 'aren't you early? I thought it didn't open till lunchtime.'

Emily shook her head. 'Dave said now that I'm out of school, I can start coming in early to clean. It means an extra ten hours a week, Brooke. If I can put all the money in the bank, then maybe I can go to Cedar this autumn anyway.'

The hope in her eyes was bright. Brooke didn't have the heart to extinguish it, to point out to her beloved younger sister that—no matter how many hours she worked this summer—Cedar College in the autumn would be beyond their budget. She gave Emily a hug. 'I hope so too, darling,' she said, and hated herself as she said it for feeding this impossible dream.

Emily would adjust, she told herself. At any rate, it wasn't as if she wouldn't be going to college at all. She'd soon accustom herself to the local one, and staying here in town would have advantages, too. She wouldn't be leaving all her friends, and she could still live at home.

Brooke glanced down at the floor. Of course, she thought wryly, Emily might not think of living at Oakley as an advantage, as long as Tara was around . . .

Emily poured herself another glass of orange juice and

gulped it. 'I'd better be going,' she said.

'Wait just a minute and I'll drive you,' offered Brooke. She flipped through the mail piled on the counter, and stopped at a cream-coloured envelope. It was of heavy bond paper, obviously expensive, with a return address that made her stomach queasy. That, she told herself, was a nonsensical way to react to a name on an envelope. Why would Tyler Marshall be writing to her now?

He had sent flowers to her father's funeral three months ago. She hadn't expected it of him; she certainly hadn't wanted the flowers. But if it made him feel better to acknowledge Elliot's death, that was all right by her. It was a small enough gesture, after all, for the man who had done so much for him.

So she had done the polite thing and sent a stiff little note thanking him for the thought. But she certainly hadn't invited this, she told herself, staring down at the cream-coloured envelope.

If he believed that her note had been an invitation to start up a correspondence—well, Brooke thought, I'll soon tell him I'm not interested in a pen-pal. I'm through with Tyler Marshall. That was all over with four years ago, when Ty left town . . .

She put the letter in her handbag. She'd open it later, when sharp-eyed Emily wasn't around.

'No, thanks,' said Emily. 'I'll ride my bike. I'm going to the club after work, for a tennis lesson.'

'Dave's paying you wages, and charging you for lessons?' Brooke said drily. 'Wouldn't it be easier if he just kept his money?'

Emily blushed a little, then said, in a rush, 'He's not charging me any more. He told me he knew we couldn't afford lessons, but that I was too good a player to lose.'

That was true enough, Brooke admitted. Dave, whose business was hamburgers but whose first love was tennis, had told her more than once that Emily was championship material. Cedar College thought so too; the athletics department there had offered her a scholarship based on her skill at the sport. Unfortunately, even with the grant, the tuition was more than Brooke would be able to afford.

And it was also true that tennis lessons didn't fit easily into the budget any more. They were doing all right on Brooke's salary, but there wasn't much left for extras. 'Sometimes I think we should resign from the club and ask for a refund on our dues,' she said, almost to herself.

Emily was horrified. 'No, please, Brooke! I have to keep up my skills, and you said yourself that since Daddy had paid for the whole year, we might as well enjoy it this summer, at least, before we're really poverty-stricken.'

'I have a question. What's poverty-stricken?' asked Tara, from the floor, where she was still aimlessly rubbing at the orange juice.

'Something that we're not,' Brooke said. 'As long as we still have Oakley and each other.' She pulled Tara to her feet. 'Wash yourself off and put the rest of your soggy cereal down the garbage disposal, and I'll take you to school.'

'Mrs Wilson used to clear up,' Tara informed her loftily. 'Why don't we still have Mrs Wilson?'

'Because we're poverty-stricken,' said Emily. 'You can talk all you like about Oakley, Brooke, but how long can we afford to keep it? It's a white elephant.'

Brooke bit her lip. 'It is our home, Emily. We have to live somewhere, and Oakley is paid for. And you know how important it is for the three of us to stick together. Remember how Mom used to say that there's nothing in the world that can defeat three Carlisles, if they put their minds to it?'

Emily's mouth twisted. 'I remember. Well, let's put our minds to restoring the family fortunes, shall we?' She didn't wait for an answer. A couple of minutes later, Brooke saw her sister's bicycle coast down the driveway.

Tara looked troubled. 'I don't remember, Brooke,' she confided.

'Of course you don't, darling. I'm sorry.' She gave this smallest sister an impulsive hug. Tara had been only two when their mother died. Sometimes it seemed to Brooke like a very long time since she'd gone, but on other days it felt as if her mother were still there, at Oakley, just in another room. Occasionally Brooke thought she could almost smell her mother's perfume. She had always smelled like jonquils, Brooke realised. Perhaps that was what made spring Brooke's favourite time of year.

At any rate, she told herself, she would not sacrifice Oakley. That, after all, was why her mother had left the house to Brooke instead of to Elliot. 'Good thing too,' she muttered.. 'Or Alison would have it now, along with nearly everything else he ever owned . . . '

Just the idea of her lovely but hard stepmother owning Oakley was enough to send cold shivers up Brooke's spine. Emily had called her the Duchess, and the girl hadn't been far wrong. The woman had been scarcely older than Brooke herself, but she had loved playing the part of the lady of the manor. Brooke would never forget the look on Alison's face, shortly after she had married Elliot, when she had mentioned her plans to redecorate the house, and Elliot had told her casually that she couldn't, because Oakley belonged to Brooke. It had been the first time, but not the last, that Brooke had met a look of hate from Alison Carlisle . . .

It had been bad enough, having Alison living at Oakley, lording it over them all and pretending to mother little Tara, while Elliot was alive. But the mere thought of Alison owning everything that Brooke's mother had inherited, cared for, and added to, was too horrible to think about.

I should be thankful, Brooke thought, that she left before he died. Otherwise I'd have had to evict her.

Enough of this, she told herself. Funny how the mere sight of Tyler Marshall's name could bring those awful old memories back in a flood. Or perhaps it wasn't so odd, she mused. For Tyler had been a part of that period in their lives—the Alison Era, Emily called it. If Tyler had still been in Oakley Mills, Elliot Carlisle's business would not have failed. But Ty had been gone by then, and Carlisle Products had crashed, taking the family fortune with it. And without his business, deserted by his young wife, there had been nothing left for Elliot to live for.

No wonder Ty had sent flowers, Brooke thought. After

everything my father did for him, he must feel just a little guilty that he was the one who indirectly caused it all.

But there was no sense in dwelling on the past; she had to earn a living. 'Come on, Tara,' she said, 'or we'll both be late.'

Tara looked less than enthusiastic, but she retrieved her book-bag and went out to the garage.

Brooke stopped the car at the end of the curving driveway and looked back at Oakley. Emily was right, she thought. The house was too big for the three of them. But it was home, this massive L-shaped pile of rough-surfaced brick, with its beamed ceilings, and diamond-paned casement windows and ornate wood carvings. Besides, she thought, if she decided to sell Oakley, who would buy it?

She answered her own question. The same sort of people who had bought the house just down the block and split it up into the Remington Arms apartments. And that, she swore to herself, I will not allow to happen to Oakley.

A woman waved from the front gate of the Remington Arms, and Brooke braked. 'Do you want a ride down-town, Jane?' she called.

'You're a saint!' Jane called back.

'Tara, would you get in the back seat, please?'

'Why?' Tara asked reasonably. 'I was here first.' But she obediently slid out of the car and held the door for Jane, who was carrying a box of green plants.

'What are those for?' asked Brooke. 'Don't tell me—you're starting a greenhouse.' She turned a corner and headed for Tara's school.

Jane laughed. 'No, but I thought they'd look nice in that high window in the Friends' shop at the library. It will soften the place up a bit, you know.'

'And you'll just happen to stick price tags on them, so if the patrons see ones they like——Here you go, Tara the Terrific.' Brooke offered her cheek for Tara's some-what sticky kiss. 'Have a good day in school. I'll see you at the library this afternoon.'

'It still isn't fair,' muttered Tara, and went off towards the playground.

Jane lifted an eyebrow. 'Do I smell a revolution?'

'Only a minor rebellion. Since Emily's graduation last week, spring fever has hit Tara hard.'

'Think positive. Two weeks into summer, she'll be bored to tears.'

'That's positive?'

Jane laughed. 'Well, perhaps not. I don't know how you handle it, Brooke. You're only twenty-five yourself, and you're mothering a nine-year-old and riding herd on a teenager——'

'Emily doesn't need a supervisor. She's a good, solid kid.'

'I know she is, but——' Whatever was causing the doubt in Jane's voice, she didn't expand on it. Instead, she brushed a fleck of dust off the shiny leaf of an ivy plant and said, 'If these sell well in the Friends' shop, perhaps we should try a full-fledged plant sale. We could call it—oh, I don't know. Love in Bloom, perhaps.'

Brooke groaned. 'Please, Jane! I haven't recovered from your last brainstorm yet—Brooke's Books.'

Jane shrugged. 'We needed a little public relations, and a book review column in the local paper was the best way to get it.'

'Which reminds me,' said Brooke, 'I haven't written it yet this week.' She parked the little car in the director's spot behind the old stone building. 'Unless you'd like to do it for me? As the president of the Friends of the Library . . .'

Jane grinned and slid out of the car, holding the box of plants carefully. 'That's the director's job, Miss Carlisle,' she said, with assumed humility.

'Along with a lot of other things, in a library this size.' The back door was already unlocked. Brooke pushed it open.

The building was old, its limestone exterior stained and weathered with the dust, rain, and grime of a hundred years. It had been built to the specifications of another era, when coal for heating was cheap and high ceilings

were necessary to keep the summer heat from suffocating
the librarians. The result was that now Brooke was always
skimping on the rest of the budget to pay the heating and
cooling costs.

A new building, Brooke thought longingly. Once, she
had thought they would build the new library. She had
been assistant director then, just out of library school and
ready to set the world on fire. The director, whose ideas
seemed as though they sprang from another century, had
not approved the prospective move from the old conven-
tional building to a new, sprawling, single-storey media
centre. She had retired in fury when the board directed
her to look into the possibility, and so Brooke had stepped
into the directorship. Some still said it was because her
father had been the main fund-raiser behind the drive for
the new building.

But before the funds were raised, the bottom had
dropped out of the Carlisle family business, throwing
dozens of people out of work, and the resulting ripples
through the town's economy had brought the fund drive
to a grinding halt. The plant had limped along for another
year, functioning at a fraction of capacity, and closed for
good shortly before Elliot's death. Now, only Brooke's
job remained as a reminder . . .

'Brooke?' asked Jane. 'Are you all right?'

'Sure.' She looked around with a critical eye, and
shivered. It was cold inside the heavy walls; spring's warm
sunlight didn't stand a chance of getting through. But
wait till summer arrived, she thought. Once the heat built
up in those stone walls, it would be a continual battle to
keep the place below the temperature of a sauna. 'I was
just thinking about how much I hate this place.'

'Well, be careful who you say that to. Would you help
me get these plants into the Friends' room? My key is
buried in the bottom of my handbag.'

Brooke found hers and unlocked the grating that served
as a door when no volunteer was on duty. This room
seemed to be the only bright and cheery one in the whole
building, she thought.

It had been her idea in the first place to set up a little

shop staffed by volunteer members of the Friends of the
Library group, where used books that the library no
longer needed could be sold. Jane had taken over from
there, and now the Friends' room also offered bookplates,
embossed stationery, greeting cards, pens and pencils for
sale. And plants, Brooke added, watching Jane set the
greenery out to show to the best advantage.

'You know,' Jane said thoughtfully, in the tone of voice
that Brooke had learned to be wary of, 'I was thinking
the other day that with summer coming up, a soda
fountain would do a booming business around here.'

'Not in the library!' Brooke announced.

'I know,' said Jane regretfully. 'The kids would smear
ice cream all over the books. But isn't it a lovely idea? In
the middle of a heat wave, you could walk down the hall
and get a strawberry sundae.'

'Make it a strawberry daiquiri and I'd be more inclined
to approve the idea,' laughed Brooke. 'Do me a favour,
Jane. Don't tear out any walls without my approval.'

'Would I do a thing like that?' Jane sounded horrified.

'Of course you would.'

'Well, perhaps you're right. But only if it benefited the
library. Here, have a plant to put on your desk!' She put
a sprig of ivy in a plastic pot into Brooke's hand.

'Why?' Brooke asked warily. 'Don't you have room for
this one?'

'Not exactly. Besides, in your office it will be like
another advertisement for the shop.' Jane put on the lapel
pin that marked her as a volunteer. *I'M A FRIEND,* it
said.

Brooke looked at the ivy doubtfully, then carried it
back to her office and set it on the corner of her desk.
She didn't feel like arguing with Jane today.

The library's mail was already piled in the centre of the
blotter, where the caretaker had left it. She started going
through it. Most of it went straight into the wastepaper
basket, and Brooke was uneasily aware that this morning
she was not paying full attention to her job. Finally she
reached into her handbag for the cream-coloured envelope.
The sooner she face up to Tyler Marshall's letter, the

sooner she could get back to work.

She handled it carefully, as if afraid it would burn her. After all these years, she thought she had put the memories behind her, but now, all the old pain seemed to boil up inside her again as if it had just been yesterday.

She had thought she loved him, once. For a few weeks she had even worn his ring—a tiny chip of a diamond set in a fragile band. His pride had forbidden him to put himself in debt for a larger stone. She had thought it a little silly of him—after all, her father would have been delighted to make him a loan—but there was no arguing with Ty Marshall's pride. She had learned that early on.

He had been Elliot's chief assistant then, the one who did most of the day-to-day work in keeping the Carlisle plant running at full production. Brooke had faint memories of him, hanging around Oakley and making himself indispensable, from when she was little. Even before Tara was born he had been there, she thought. She had never paid much attention to him until she started working in the plant office herself, in the summers when she came home from college. Then she had quickly become aware of the young man with the eyes that could change from silvery-grey to black in an instant. He had had a way of looking at her that had made her feel all woman . . .

Enough of that, Brooke told herself crossly. There was no point in remembering how she had felt about him, or how pleased Elliot had been when they had announced their engagement. Ty had been the son Elliot had always wanted. Despite his youth, Ty had practically taken over Carlisle Products.

That was the worst of it, she thought. He had been good at his job, and if he had stayed Carlisle Products would have made a fortune on the strength of Ty Marshall's new discoveries.

How innocent I was, Brooke thought. I believed I knew what love was. I didn't know that all we shared was sexual attraction. I'm so very lucky that I found out when I did that it went no deeper than that for either of us.

She didn't feel lucky, she thought grimly, and fought against the wave of sickening memory that threatened her. She would never forget the look of guilt on Tyler's face the day she had found him with Alison in his arms. It was something she would never be able to erase from her mind. Within a week, Ty had left Oakley Mills for good. He had gone to work for another office supply firm, and less than a year later he made the discoveries that had destroyed the market for Carlisle Products.

'Typewriter ribbons,' said Brooke, under her breath. 'Who would have thought Dad could go broke manufacturing the same typewriter ribbon that made him rich?'

Well, Mr Tyler Marshall, she thought, and ripped the envelope open. We'll just see what you want this time.

The letter left her unenlightened. It was crisp, formal, polite, informing her that he would be in Oakley Mills on Wednesday, 15 May, and would call to see her.

'No, thanks,' Brooke muttered. 'I shall be out of town, even if I have to make a special trip.' Except that today was Wednesday. He would be here today.

She glanced at the postmark. The letter had been mailed only two days ago; Ty, apparently, was willing to take his chances on finding her. Either that, or he was certain she would want so badly to see him that she would toss to the winds any plans she had made . . .

Perhaps it would be best if she found out what it was he wanted. What harm could it do to see him? In a way, she wanted to know what the years, and the acquisition of money, had done for him. And what, she wondered, would he think when he saw her?

She glanced at the photograph of herself, with her father, Emily and Tara, that stood on the corner of her desk. She was wearing the same lime-green suit today; it skimmed her slender figure and accented the darker green of her eyes. Her honey-blonde hair was loose and wavy around her shoulders. She hadn't changed much, physically, in the last four years, and she was a self-assured woman now, instead of a foolish girl. Yes, she thought, satisfied, she could still set a man back on his heels. If Ty expected to see a woman who regretted what she had given up four years ago—well, he'd be in for a surprise.

She put the letter back in her desk drawer and started

on her routine work. It was just another day in the library, broken up by complaints from a couple of patrons and arguments between staff members. They were currently short of two employees, and as the budget frowned on hiring anyone extra at the moment, Brooke found herself filling in on whatever job needed doing.

That was why she was at the desk in the reference department, helping a student with research on capital punishment for a speech he was giving, when Tyler Marshall came in.

Both telephone lines were blinking impatiently at her. The woman in front of the desk was shifting from one foot to the other. The student was reading out a list of magazines he needed to see, and Brooke was writing them down.

There was no reason why she should have looked up just then. Ty Marshall had made no sound as he crossed the carpeted room. He had not said a word. Yet in the middle of a phrase, Brooke looked up through the crowd around the desk, and saw him.

I wouldn't have recognised him if I hadn't expected to see him here, she thought. He looks so old——No, she corrected. He doesn't look old at all. He looks timeless, and dangerous . . .

Now why did I think that? she wondered. For there was nothing about him that was actively threatening. He looked calm, mildly interested in his surroundings. And the only thing that had changed about him was his hair. When he had left Oakley Mills, it had been black. Now it was startlingly, flamboyantly, silver. Not grey, not white, but silver.

It was the hair that had made her think at first that he had grown old. She could see, on second glance, how wrong she had been. His face was unlined and tanned, his eyes bright, his shoulders square, his eyebrows and lashes still dark. Of course, she thought. He was only thirty-three.

'Miss,' the woman said finally, 'if you'd hand me the price guide for old bottles, I'll get out of your way.'

Brooke gulped and coloured. What a wonderful way to

start, she cursed herself, to stand there and stare at him like a lovestruck kid! She handed over the requested book, and turned towards the student. 'If you'll just give me that list,' she said, 'I'll order the issues you need. We don't carry all of those magazine titles.' The telephone lights were still blinking. 'I have to answer these questions first,' she added, looking up at Tyler Marshall, and hated herself because it sounded like an apology.

He shrugged. 'I'll wait,' he said. He took a chair near the desk, leaned his elbows on the arms of it, tented his fingers together, and watched her with steady concentration.

She tried to ignore his scrutiny, but she couldn't. She was fiercely aware of him, sitting there silently motionless. It made her angry, that he had the gall to sit there and stare at her, and when she turned back to him her eyes were fiercely green. 'Well? Are you satisfied with what you see?' she asked. 'What do you want?'

'Could we discuss it in private, perhaps?' he murmured.

'I didn't think you were merely paying a social call,' she snapped, 'or I'd have ordered up the tea tray. I have nothing to say to you that can't be said right here.'

'In private,' he said. It was very soft, and it didn't sound in the least like a command.

But Brooke found herself on her feet. 'I'll have to get someone to cover for me,' she said.

'I have all the time in the world.'

A few minutes later she led him into her office. He closed the door, and Brooke felt panic rise in her. She hadn't been alone with him, closed into a room like this, since the day she had thrown her engagement ring at him——

He picked up the picture frame on the corner of her desk and looked at it closely. 'Your father had lost a lot of weight.'

'He'd been ill for a long time. That was taken just a few weeks before he died.'

'The girls have changed.'

'We all have. I don't have all day to chat, Tyler. What is it you want?'

He moved his chair closer to her desk. 'I understand you inherited your father's stock in Carlisle Products.'

So, it was business. Well, you didn't expect it to be anything else, did you? Brooke asked herself. She shifted some papers around on her desk. 'I'm touched that you chose to pay your condolences in person,' she said sweetly.

'Are you? In that case, you may consider that I've offered them.'

Somehow she didn't feel she had won that round. 'As for the stock,' she went on, 'your information isn't quite correct. Of course, I don't know exactly where you got it,' she smiled up at him, 'but you can tell Alison she was wrong.'

'To be just a little more precise,' he added, 'your father owned sixty per cent of the company. Shortly before he died, he transferred one-fourth of his holdings to Alison, as part of their separation agreement. The rest was split at his death between you, Emily and Tara.'

She tried to conceal her surprise. He'd hit that on the nose. And so what? she told herself irritably. Alison might have known the details, even though she had left before Elliot died. Or it could have been a lucky guess. It had been the logical way to divide the stock. The only problem was, Brooke thought, that by the time it was divided, it was next to worthless.

'Wills are a matter of public record,' Tyler pointed out. 'And your father's was an interesting one. He named you as guardian for Emily and Tara until they're of age.'

'So what? I can't see that it's any of your concern.'

'That means that you control their shares as well as your own. Forty-five per cent of Carlisle Products is in your hands.'

'At the risk of being redundant, why should it matter to you?'

'I want that stock,' he said.

'Why? As a souvenir of past joys?' The words were out before she thought. She felt herself flushing again.

Ty smiled grimly. 'No. I have souvenirs enough. I'll pay twenty dollars a share for it today.'

Brooke gasped. 'Alison's portion was valued at a

hundred a share in the separation agreement.'

Tyler shrugged. 'That was before the public found out how much trouble your father was in. I can't help it if the market for office-product companies, especially this one, has gone to hell in the last year. I'll give you twenty. It's probably worth ten.'

'Don't do me any favours,' she said baldly. 'If it's barely worth the paper it's printed on, then why do you want it?'

'My reasons are my business.'

'I suppose you want to buy me out so you can boast of giving me charity!'

The accusation glanced off him. 'Shouldn't you check with your sisters to see how they feel?' he asked.

'The Carlisles stand together. We're not interested in turning our father's company over to you.'

'That attitude sounds familiar,' he mused. 'It was almost precisely what your father told me, when he decided not to modernise the plant.' He rose, and replaced the chair against the wall. 'Perhaps it's only fair to warn you, Brooke, that I already own a considerable portion of the rest of the firm.'

'Alison's share, I suppose,' Brooke said bitterly. 'I hope she held you up for it.'

Tyler smiled. 'I see no reason to tell you where I made my purchases or how much I paid. I've made you an offer.'

'Get out!' she snapped.

That imperious dark eyebrow raised again. 'But, my dear Brooke,' he said softly, 'this is a public place, funded with taxpayer's money. And since I'm now a resident of Oakley Mills, I have every right to be here.'

A resident? Why on earth would he be coming back to Oakley Mills?

'But since it bothers you to see me,' he said, 'I'll stop another time to apply for my library card. I'll be seeing you again, Brooke. We have so much in common— including our co-ownership of Carlisle Products.'

CHAPTER TWO

It was a bluff, thought Brooke. Tyler Marshall didn't own any of that stock—except Alison's, perhaps—because no one would have sold it to him. There were only two other partners; one of them had been Elliot's banker, the other his attorney. They both knew how suddenly Tyler had left Oakley Mills, leaving Elliot and the business in the lurch. Neither of them would betray Elliot's memory by selling that stock, especially once they knew that Brooke was standing firm.

And even Alison wouldn't be fool enough to actually sell her stock to Tyler, Brooke thought. She'd hang on to every last share, knowing that just because he wanted it, it might be worth more than its simple cash value.

Which brought her back to the starting point. There was no way that Tyler would get his hands on any more of that stock unless he first persuaded her to sell hers. And that, Brooke was determined, would never happen. It had all been a bluff that he was trying to pull, to con her into selling the forty-five per cent of the stock that the three sisters owned. He knew that once he owned that, it would be no great trick to persuade the banker and the attorney to sell out.

'You'd better watch out, Alison,' muttered Brooke. If he got what he was after, he wouldn't need Alison's fifteen per cent at all, no matter what the price.

Well, he won't get my shares, she resolved.

And then she started to wonder. Why did he want them, anyway? Why did he want to own Carlisle Products? The factory was defunct, closed, nothing but a mass of obsolete equipment stacked in a dusty building. The merchandise that remained when the plant closed had been sold at a loss, just to save the warehouse expense.

The customer lists were outdated, the goodwill gone. What was there left to buy?

It puzzled her, and tugged at the corners of her mind for the rest of the day. She found no solution to the problem, only more questions, and she finally concluded that whatever Tyler's reasons were, it made no difference to her.

It was raining when the library closed for the day, one of those sudden spring showers that seem to come from nowhere. Tara was sitting on a window-seat in the reference room, waiting patiently for Brooke, watching the raindrops trickle down the plate glass. She had been there since school finished, and she didn't even look up when Brooke came over.

Brooke stood there silently for a few moments, watching the little girl. It was time to start looking for a babysitter for Tara for the summer, she thought wearily. She was certainly too young to stay at home by herself. Last summer, Emily had kept an eye on her while Brooke was at work, but this year that wouldn't be possible; Emily would be far too busy herself. And of course, last summer their father had still been alive, and Tara had felt important because she was keeping him company and making sure that he was all right, never realising that he was also looking after her.

What am I going to do with her this summer? Brooke wondered. A child should be running and playing and having a good time, not sitting around the library, watching it rain.

Don't borrow trouble, she told herself finally. Surely, in the next couple of weeks, she could find an answer? 'Time to go, Tara,' she said. 'Shall we run past the club and pick up Emily? She'll get drenched if she rides her bike home.'

Tara thought it over for a minute, and Brooke regretted phrasing it as a question. 'I guess so,' the child said.

'The empathy you have for your fellow creatures is touching,' Brooke told her.

'I have a question,' announced Tara. 'What's empathy?'

'Tell you what, I'll get you a dictionary for your birthday.'

They found Emily in the club lounge, drinking iced water and listening closely as her coach criticised her form on court that day. 'See?' said Tara. 'She didn't get wet at all.'

The coach looked up. 'I'll buy you a drink, Brooke,' he offered, getting to his feet.

'Thanks, Dave. Just a cup of coffee, though—anything stronger would knock me off my feet after the day I've had.'

'Gee,' said Emily. 'How do you rate? He wouldn't even buy me a soda.'

Dave saw no humour in the remark. 'That's because water is better for you after exercise,' he said sternly. 'It would be better yet if you drank it at room temperature.'

Emily looked at her water glass with horror. 'You expect me to leave out the ice?'

'No. I expect you'll do what you like. But it would be better for you. Bad day, Brooke?'

He held her chair, and Brooke sank gratefully into the deep, plush seat. Dave Sheridan was one of her favourite people. He had wanted to be a professional tennis player, but a knee injury early in his career had put paid to that dream. Now he ran a chain of fast-food restaurants for a living, and doubled as the tennis pro at the country club each summer, teaching the little kids how to hold a racquet. He had infinite patience and striking grace on the court. Without a racquet, he was slightly awkward and ill at ease. He never quite seemed to know what to do with his hands, and his sandy hair was always rumpled where he nervously ran his fingers through it.

Brooke smiled up at him with genuine fondness. She felt she had known Dave ages, though it had actually been only a couple of years. Dave had come to Oakley Mills long after Ty had left——But she had decided not to think about Ty any more, she reminded herself. She would think about Dave instead. Some day she would probably marry Dave. Everybody expected it. Some day, after Emily was settled at college, and Tara was a little older.

I love my sisters dearly, Brooke thought. But sometimes I just feel so old, and so responsible. And so tired of having all the weight to carry by myself.

Emily was all right. She was a good, solid girl, who had a tremendous future. But then Brooke looked across the table at Tara, who was stirring a soft drink with her straw, and felt a stab of guilt. It wasn't Tara's fault that she needed someone to look after her. And if not Brooke, then who? Emily was too young. The only other possibility was Alison . . .

And I'd send Tara to an orphanage before I allowed that she-monster to get her hands on my little sister again, Brooke thought.

She didn't realise she was showing her feelings until Dave said quietly, 'I'm glad I'm not the spoon you're squeezing. It must have been a rough day.'

'That isn't the half of it.' She noticed Emily watching her with interest. 'Em, why don't you take your things down to the locker room? I'll be ready to go in a few minutes.'

Emily got up unwillingly. 'If you're trying to get rid of us so you can talk to Dave,' she began, 'you could just give me the car keys and I'll go on home to start dinner.'

'Not a bad idea,' Dave agreed.

'Who said I was trying to get rid of you?' Brooke asked. 'Besides, how would I get home? I'm not planning to ride your bike.'

Emily shrugged. 'Come on, Tara,' she said. 'Let's leave the lovebirds alone for a couple of minutes.'

'Speaking of lovebirds . . . ' said Dave, as soon as the girls had vanished.

'What's up? You sound concerned.'

'I am, a little. I probably made too big a deal of it, but when I got out to the court today, Emily was already there talking to Bart Tipton.'

'Bart . . . Oh, the juvenile delinquent, with the ever-present cigarette?'

'That's the one.'

'I've had trouble with him at the library. What was he doing here, for heaven's sake? This is still a private club.'

'That's what I asked. And Emily told me that Bart was her guest and I should mind my own business.'

Brooke let out a long, slow whistle. 'What happened to him?'

'He hung around for a bit, but when I kept Emily too busy on the court to pay attention to him, he drifted off.'

Brooke nibbled at her bottom lip. 'I think I'd better have a chat with one Emily Carlisle concerning her choice of friends,' she decided.

'Well, she'll know I ratted on her, of course. I don't suppose there's any way around that.'

'I'm glad you told me, Dave.'

'Yeah. I just wish I'd known it sooner. It's been going on for a while, I'm sure of it.' He looked at her with concern. 'What are you going to do, Brooke?'

'I don't know.'

Dave sighed. 'I like Emily a lot.' he said, 'but I have to admit I'm glad that I'm not her guardian. I don't envy you the job a bit, Brooke.'

Brooke forced a smile. She'd been sitting there worrying about Tara, and thinking that all was well with Emily. It just goes to show, she told herself, that there's no vacation from this job. And no one who's very willing to help, either.

A group of men came in from the club's equipment shop. They were all wet to varying degrees; most had towels draped around their necks to absorb the water that dripped from their hair. They seemed to be having a good time, though, laughing as they gathered around the bar.

'Darn fools,' said Dave. 'They must have been at the far end of the course when it started to pour. As if they couldn't see that it was bound to rain today.'

'At least it was warm.' Brooke didn't pay any more attention until a shadow fell across her coffee-cup.

'What a pleasant surprise,' said a deep voice. 'I didn't expect to see you here.'

She looked up. 'Likewise,' she said coolly. 'I'm here

because I'm a member of this club, Tyler. Can you say the same?'

The barb glanced off him. That was new, she thought. In the old days, Ty Marshall would have stammered and apologised. He had never seemed to like the club. She wondered, now, if he had felt uncomfortable there because he hadn't paid his own way in. Then she told herself crossly not to waste her time trying to analyse Ty's motives.

'Not quite,' he admitted. 'I'm a temporary member until the board acts on my application. Not that it's in doubt, of course, since I'm merely transferring from another club. Would you like to see my ID card?'

So he had meant it, then, about moving back to Oakley Mills. The thought made her uneasy, and she struck out, saying tartly, 'What on earth is this place coming to?'

Tyler's grey eyes hardened to cold steel, and for an instant, Brooke was actually a tiny bit afraid of him. That was new too, she thought. More than the colour of his hair had changed in the years since he had left Oakley Mills.

Abruptly, the charm was back, masking the danger that she had seen in his eyes. But it didn't fool Brooke. He's like a chameleon, she thought. And just because a chameleon turns all sorts of pretty colours, it doesn't make him any less a reptile. Remember that, she reminded herself. Ty cannot be trusted.

'Now that you've had a chance to think about my offer, Brooke——' he said smoothly.

'The answer is still no.'

He shook his head. 'I beg your pardon,' he said. 'Obviously I've gotten some bad information, if you can afford to whistle that proposition down the wind. It's a matter of fifteen thousand dollars altogether.'

'You're right,' Brooke said calmly. 'You've been misled. By Alison's standards I'm probably next door to the poorhouse, but actually we're doing quite well.' She pushed her coffee-cup aside.

'I can see in that case that I'll have to improve the price,' he said. He looked thoughtfully off into the distance, over the brilliant green of the golf course, newly washed by the rain. Then he said, 'This will be my final offer, you understand.'

'Good.' She saw Emily and Tara come back into the lounge. 'You're finally getting the message that I'm not interested.'

Ty didn't seem to hear. 'Thirty dollars a share, Brooke. I'll be at the hotel for the next couple of hours, if you're interested. I'm staying there.' He put a business card on the table.

'Don't stay in all night waiting for me to call.'

'I won't,' he said gently. 'That's why you shouldn't be stubborn about it. That's quite a chunk of money to play with.'

'Tainted money.' Brooke's voice was cold. 'Let's go home, girls.'

There was a dead silence in the car. Brooke could feel Emily looking at her, and she bit her lip, trying to find a way to broach the subject of Bart Tipton without bringing Emily's wrath down on Dave. She felt like a coward, but she decided to let it wait till after dinner.

But as soon as they were in the kitchen at Oakley Manor, and Brooke was browning pork chops, Emily found her voice.

'That was Ty Marshall you were talking too at the club, wasn't it?'

'It certainly was.'

'Did he say he was willing to pay thirty dollars a share for our Carlisle Products shares?'

'That's what he said.'

'And you turned him down?' Emily's voice was hoarse. 'Brooke, that's thousands of dollars! My share alone would send me through college. A worthless piece of paper, and you won't sell it?'

'In the first place, your share would barely see you through your first year at Cedar, Emily. It's not a fortune, and Cedar is expensive.'

'But it's something! We thought that stock was worthless. It's like finding money!'

'Always assuming that he could come up with the cash.'

'Come on, Brooke. Didn't you ever listen to Dad
talking about how Ty made it big? To Ty Marshall, that
sort of money is pocket change. You must have some
idea of what those patents of his are worth.'

'As a matter of fact, I do. That still doesn't mean he
could pay cash.' Brooke flipped the chops in the frying
pan and turned to face Emily. 'And the other side of that
question is, why does a man like Tyler Marshall suddenly
want to own Carlisle Products?'

'Who cares?' asked Emily. 'As long as he's willing to
pay for the privilege, he can bulldoze the place, and I'll
stand on the sidewalk and cheer.'

'He put Dad out of business.'

'Brooke, it isn't as if he meant to! The man made a
better typewriter ribbon, and the world beat a path to his
door. You can't hold that against him.'

That much was true, Brooke had to admit. She couldn't
really blame Tyler Marshall for the fact that the market
had changed. If he hadn't been the one to make the
breakthrough, someone else would have, and Carlisle
Products would still have suffered.

But of course, Emily didn't know it all, Brooke reflected.
She didn't know about Tyler and Alison, and why
Brooke's engagement had been abruptly broken off. Emily
had been too young to understand it all. She hadn't been
the one who had walked into the quiet solarium at Oakley
Manor on a summer afternoon four years ago and found
Ty on the loveseat there with the young Mrs Carlisle,
kissing her with a desperate passion that had almost
nauseated Brooke. Emily hadn't seen the naked guilt on
his face, and the horror—not at what he had done,
Brooke thought, but that he had been caught doing it——

It had been four long years, but Brooke remembered
every dreadful word they had said that afternoon. But
Emily knew none of it, and Brooke wasn't going to tell
her.

She said, firmly, 'I will not even talk to Ty Marshall
about that stock, Emily. Now that's the end of the
discussion.'

'Well, I will!' flashed Emily. 'A third of it's mine, and I'll——'

'You can't.' Brooke didn't like the way she sounded, but there was no other choice. 'I'm your guardian. Until you're twenty-one, you can't sell it without my permission.'

The fire in Emily's eyes was almost hatred. She stormed out of the room, and Brooke sighed as she heard the stairs squeak under Emily's weight as she took them at a run. She was on her way to her room to cry it out, Brooke thought. She remembered being seventeen. It was tough, even without the added complication of a sister who refused to see things the same way. But Emily wouldn't understand . . .

She stared out of the window at the gathering dusk, and remembered Alison's throaty purr that afternoon four years ago, when she had looked up to see Brooke in the doorway. 'My goodness,' she had said, in that sultry voice. 'Your young man got a bit carried away, Brooke. He's so impulsive. Don't hold him responsible . . . ' She had still been in Ty's arms then, her orange-nailed fingers caressing the back of his neck. And Ty had made no move to free himself.

Brooke had turned and fled, trying to outrun the horrible scene. Ty had caught up with her in the hallway, grabbing her arm and swinging her around to face him.

He was breathing hard. Brooke wondered if it was because of Alison's kisses. 'Take your hands off me!' she had cried.

He pushed her into her father's small study and shut the door. 'Brooke, please—I swear to you——'

'What? That I was imagining things? That you really weren't kissing her at all? Ty, don't act like an idiot!' Her voice cracked.

'Trust me, Brooke——' He had gone white.

'I'm not a fool, Tyler. I know what I saw.'

'No, you don't. Brooke, I can't explain what happened. You have to take my word for it—you must——'

She had stood there for a long moment, wanting to believe him. But the guilt she had seen on his face, when he realised she was standing in the doorway, rose up to haunt her.

My fiancé, she thought, was in there kissing my stepmother . . . and what would he do next autumn, when Brooke went back to college to finish her final year? Would she ever be able to trust him again?

Slowly her pride reasserted itself. She must have been mistaken about her feelings for him, she told herself. It wasn't possible for her to love a man who was capable of behaving like this, a man who refused to account for his actions. It meant to Brooke that he could think of no satisfactory explanation, no story that she might accept.

Very well, she thought. If he would not explain, then that was all there was to be said about it. She would not let him see how hurt she was. It was only her pride, after all. How fortunate she was that they hadn't rushed into marriage!

She had stared at his shirt collar where Alison's lipstick had made a fiery smudge. 'You don't need to give me any explanations, Tyler.'

His eyes glowed silvery-grey, as relief hit him. 'Then you do trust me, Brooke——'

'No,' she cut in, coldly deliberate. 'I mean that nothing you could say would convince me. So take your damned ring and get the hell out of my life!' She pulled the diamond chip from her finger and flung it full into his face.

He had been standing there, looking stunned, when she pushed past him to the door.

She had not told her father the truth. She had explained merely that she and Ty had thought better of the idea of a long engagement. She could not say more; she refused to destroy her father's trust in Alison.

He wouldn't have believed me anyway, she thought. Alison would have explained it away.

But Elliot had not pressed for details. He had merely told her how sorry he was that she was not to marry Ty after all. She could see what he was thinking. Perhaps next year, after she had left college, they would patch up their differences. She had not disillusioned him about the

conduct of the man who had been his most valued
assistant.

That, she thought, was the hardest thing of all to
forgive Tyler for—the fact that he had betrayed her father
too. The man who had done so much for Ty, the man
who had trained and nurtured him, the man who had
treated him like a son . . .

Emily came back into the kitchen. She was carrying her
Cedar College catalogue, which she flung on the floor at
Brook's feet. Pamphlets and letters and loose pages sprayed
out of the book and scattered everywhere.

'And what's that grand gesture supposed to mean?'
asked Brooke. She stepped over the mess and turned the
heat down under the pan of peas and carrots.

'Throw it away!' Emily challenged. 'You might as
well—you've destroyed everything else that matters to me.
That stock was my last chance to go to Cedar. You don't
care about me, and what I want. After all, it's only my
future that's at stake! All you care about is your damned
Carlisle pride. Well, pride doesn't pay the electricity bill,
and it doesn't taste very good, either!'

'It isn't simply pride, Emily. Ty Marshall isn't to be
trusted. He might do anything with that business——'

'Don't you understand that I don't care? I'm sick of
being Emily Carlisle, holding up the standards that you
set for the family.'

'Emily, really!'

'You had your chance. You've got your education, and
your job. All I want is that same chance, Brooke—and
you're too blind and selfish to let me have it!' Emily burst
into furious tears.

'Emily, you don't understand.'

'I'll tell you what I understand. I understand that you
don't care what happens to me. You want me to stay
here in Oakley Mills and turn into a sour old maid like
you!'

Brooke sighed. She wasn't going to argue with that
one. From Emily's standpoint, twenty-five and unmarried
must seem like the end of the world.

'Don't you understand, Brooke? They're laughing at

us—all the hoity-toity people, at the club and everywhere
else. We're just poor trash now, not fit to associate with.
And we don't even know when to quit acting like the
wonderful Carlisles!'

'Emily! That's enough!'

Emily's hot tears turned into raging sobs that tore at
her throat. She sank into a chair at the maplewood table
and buried her face in her hands.

Brooke waited a few minutes, until the flood had
receded to an occasional hiccuping sob. The she said
softly, 'I know you wanted to go to Cedar. But I also
thought that you'd enjoy staying here, where most of
your friends are. In the end, Emily, it won't make any
difference. You'll get your education.'

Emily looked up with frustration written across her
face. 'It's more than that, Brooke. I don't mind losing the
money, but I want to do things with my life. I want to be
somebody, and I can't do that unless I have a really first-
class education.'

'The junior college here is very good.'

Emily was shaking her head. 'Not for what I want, it
isn't.'

'And that is?' asked Brooke carefully. She was cutting
up lettuce for a salad, and when Emily answered, she
almost cut herself.

'Law,' the girl said shortly.

'I see.' Brooke kept her tone carefully non-committal.

'Oh, I know that's out of the question now,' Emily said
savagely. 'But I want you to know, it isn't fair. You
wanted to be a librarian. You got it. I'm willing to work
for what I want, Brooke. I'm working longer hours than
you are.'

That was true, Brooke admitted to herself. Emily had
cheerfully worked late evenings, weekends, and every
holiday she'd had from school, all spring.

'I don't want to be a waitress all my life. And I need
all the help I can get. That stock isn't worth a dime to
me, but if Ty Marshall is fool enough to pay me for
it——'

'I see what you mean, Emily,' Brooke said slowly.

'Then you'll sell it?'

'I'll think about it.'

'That would be a sort of revenge, too,' Emily pointed out. 'He'll be stuck with it, instead of us.'

And Tyler is smart enough to know that, thought Brooke. So why does he want it so badly? So he can tell everyone at the club, after he belongs and we no longer do, that he handed over thousands of dollars out of the goodness of his heart?

I will not be one of Tyler Marshall's charities, she told herself. But for Emily's sake—wasn't that a little different?

She lifted the chops out of the pan. 'Call Tara to dinner, would you, Em?'

Emily came around the counter instead. 'I'm sorry I blew up,' she said quietly. 'I was going to be calm and adult about it——' She stooped to pick up the catalogue and loose pages.

Brooke didn't answer, but she held out her arms, and Emily, shuddering with sobs, came to her. 'I didn't mean it, about you being a sour old maid, either,' Emily sniffed. 'If it wasn't for Tara and me, some neat guy would have snapped you up by now.'

'Hmm,' murmured Brooke. 'Give me a little credit for deciding who's going to snap up whom.'

Emily gave a little choke of a laugh. 'Of course, whoever marries you has a package deal,' she said. 'You and me and Tara and Oakley! The poor guy!'

'And don't forget the Carlisle pride,' Brooke prompted. 'He'd have to live with that too. Now go call Tara before dinner gets cold.'

Emily gulped her supper and went back for the evening shift at the Burger Barn. Brooke half-heartedly answered a hundred of Tara's questions, scarcely listening to most of them, before finally getting the child settled and tucked into bed. She sat down, then, in the big living-room with a skirt of Tara's and started to let the hem down.

The child was growing so fast that it was hard to keep

her in clothes. She'd grown six inches this school year, and shed most of her baby fat. She'd be a tall, slender girl, Brooke thought, as fair in colouring as Brooke herself, and as deceptively fragile-looking as Emily. And, like Emily, she would be as strong as a steel cable, and have a will forceful enough to do anything she chose.

So Emily wanted to be an attorney. It was the first time she'd been so definite about her plans. Purposely so, Brooke understood now, for Emily was realistic about her chances of getting through seven years' training. She had known that talking about it wouldn't make it come true. Emily, she thought, had always been the pragmatic one.

My heavens, thought Brooke, I'll just be recuperating financially from that, and Tara will be ready for college. And with my luck, she'll probably choose to be a doctor!

She finished ripping out the hem of Tara's skirt, and started to pin it up again. There was some fancy braiding in the bottom of her sewing basket, she remembered. She'd sew it on to cover up the line where the old hem had been.

I wonder, she thought. Is it really true that people are talking behind our backs? Or is it just that Emily is super-sensitive? She thought back over the last few months since Elliot's death and the final closing down of the Carlisle plant, and couldn't find any change in how people had acted towards her. In any case, she told herself, it didn't matter.

What mattered, and what she was trying to avoid thinking about, was the choice she had to make tonight. Was Emily right? That money *would* be a godsend to her, it would pay for the first year of college, and it might stretch farther than that if Emily was careful.

What would her father have done? Brooke wondered. He had never said much about Ty. He had made a comment now and then about the new products, but Brooke had never been able to judge whether he was jealous, bitter, hurt, or angry at his own loss—or merely resigned to his own failure. It would break his heart, she thought, to see Tyler in possession of his beloved firm, and his daughters cheated of their birthright. Or would it? Seeing Emily struggle to get what he would gladly have given her, had he only been able to, would be worse.

Revenge isn't worth it, she thought. Not if Emily suffers. I didn't know, before, how much she was suffering.

She put Tara's skirt down in her lap, leaned back against the couch cushions, and yawned. She was so tired these days. But she would not go to bed until Emily was home. That was the least she could do. She'd call Tyler tonight at the hotel, and tell him she'd sell Emily's shares of stock. Pride, she thought, and yawned again. 'Your damned Carlisle pride,' Emily had called it. Brooke had heard that phrase before . . . Long ago, it had been. Four years ago. She had tried so hard to forget . . .

She was in the garden behind Oakley Manor, on a hot afternoon just a week after she had caught Ty with Alison in his arms. Since that moment, Brooke had spent as little time under the same roof with the woman as possible. When she couldn't avoid her, she had forced herself to be coldly civil. Alison had not appeared to notice. If she could have left Oakley, she would have gone. But it was the summer vacation, and it would have been difficult to explain to her father why she could no longer bear to live in her own home.

There had been no problem in avoiding Ty. She had seen him at the plant a couple of times, and in the distance in town. But he seemed as anxious as she to keep out of each other's way.

She fled into a social whirl, announcing to her friends that with her engagement at an end, she was free to take part in any sort of fun. They had been happy to oblige. In her first week without Ty's ring, she had dated five different men, gone to three very wild parties, laughed a bit shrilly but a great deal, drunk a little too much, kissed anyone who asked her . . .

None of it had removed Ty from her mind, and that had made her angry. So, on that blisteringly hot afternoon, she had retreated to the garden, where Alison almost never went, to take out her frustrations on the weeds in the formal flower beds. She'd been kneeling there with a trowel, perspiration soaking through her thin skirt, when Ty Marshall had come up the drive.

This time he hadn't turned aside. He came directly across the grass to her.

'If you're looking for Alison,' she said, without attempting to conceal her irritation at finding him there, 'she's in the library, eating chocolates and battling to understand a book.' She had looked up, then. 'Personally,' she added, 'I'd bet on the book winning.'

'I'm not looking for Alison,' he said. 'Don't you have any idea why I came here today, Brooke?'

'Not only do I not know,' she said loftily, 'I don't care in the least.'

'You should care.' He had moved a little closer, and she felt uncomfortable. There was a masculine smell tickling her nose, reminding her of the times when she had been much closer than this to him. The flower bed lay in the corner of a wrought-iron fence, and where he was standing, he was blocking her in.

'And you should be at work.'

'I can't work with this thing hanging between us, Brooke.'

She looked up in surprise. 'What do you mean, hanging?' she asked. 'There's nothing between us. It's over, Tyler.'

'You can't believe that what we shared is gone just because you took my ring off——'

'It's true. We never shared anything important. In fact, there's nothing about you I give a darn about any more—except your absence. If you'd move out of my way, Ty . . . ' She cut the stem of a spray of delicate scarlet gladioli and stood up, sniffing the flowers.

'And what will you do if I don't?' he asked softly.

'Then I'll walk around you, if I have to.'

'Try it,' he said. His hand locked on the wrought iron, imprisoning her against the fence. 'We're going to talk about this.'

'Oh? Have you had a chance to concoct a believable story now? You were the one who refused to explain, Tyler. You weren't willing to talk about it then, and I'm not willing to hear about it now!'

'I'm going to make you hear me out, Brooke.'

'I absolutely refuse to listen. Let me pass!' she demanded.

He repeated it, mockingly. 'Have you ever heard of "please", Miss Carlisle?' The tone of his voice made the title an insult.

'Not for the likes of you,' she said coldly. But fear made her voice unsteady, and her breath was coming rapidly.

He saw too. Beneath her thin blouse, her breasts were trembling with every breath she took. He stood there for a moment and looked at her, up and down the length of her, and then he reached out, as a curious child would have tentatively touched a toystore display, and brushed his hand down across her breast.

She hit him, with every ounce of strength she possessed. The sound of her open palm striking his face seemed to echo around the garden. Her arm stung all the way to the shoulder with the impact, and his cheek turned fiery red. But he had not flinched or moved.

'I always knew you were from the wrong side of the tracks, Ty,' she said bitterly, 'but I never realised that my father had to drag you out of the gutter!'

He sucked in a breath, and she was horrified at what she had said. The words hung in the air between them. It must have felt like a whiplash across his pride, she thought.

So what? she asked herself sullenly. He deserved to be hurt, just so he knew what it felt like.

She didn't quite see him move; all she knew was that an instant later he had seized her and was holding her so closely against him that she couldn't get her breath. She could feel every separate muscle in his body as he held her, seemingly without effort, while she struggled.

She fought, but he forced her head up, and kissed her, over and over, like a brand searing her lips. His tongue probed her mouth, hot and demanding. 'Brooke——' he said, and it was half plea, half threat.

When he let her go, she stood panting for a moment, then she spat down into the flower bed, trying futilely to rid herself of the taste of him. 'Don't ever touch me again, you clumsy ox!' she snapped. 'After what you did, you have the nerve to touch me——'

He was breathing hard too. 'What's the matter, Brooke?' he queried. 'I've certainly kissed you before.'

Not like that, her horrified brain was screaming. Not with violence, and force——

'And you let your new boy-friends kiss you. In fact, from some of the things I've heard about your behaviour this week, I wouldn't be surprised to trip over you in the middle of Main Street!'

'That's an entirely different matter.' But she was startled. How did Ty know that she'd been less restrained than usual?

'Apparently it is. You don't think I'm good enough to touch you any more, do you? But they can do anything they like!'

She said, slowly and deliberately, hardly hearing the words, 'Don't you understand, Tyler? I would never have married you. It was fun to be engaged—all the girls were. But to actually marry you?' Shudders racked her body, and she was horrified at the harsh, hateful words that poured from her. But she could not stop herself. 'You're not my type, Ty. I don't ever want to see you again. Go crawl back into your gutter!'

Her flowers had been dropped in the struggle. Now he looked down at them, crushed in the dusty path. Something in his face had hardened and tightened into a mask. 'I'll stay out of your way, Brooke,' he said. 'But first, let me tell you this. Some day I'm going to break that damned Carlisle pride of yours, just like this——' His foot went down on the delicate flowers, and ground them deliberately into the path. 'That's a promise.'

He had turned and walked off, leaving her there against the fence, looking down at the scarlet stain on the path . . .

Brooke sat up straight, shuddering. She'd almost forgotten that day; it had been too much torment to remember it. How, she had asked herself in the dark nights that followed, had she ever thought that she loved this dark and violent man?

She had not seen him again. True to his word, he had stayed out of her way. Within two days he was gone from Oakley Mills, and she was free.

It was all over, then, all past, and she was free to forget Ty Marshall and the summer she had been his fiancée.

Except, she thought, ever since that day, she had never liked the smell of gladioli much . . .

CHAPTER THREE

EMILY was late. Brooke finished the hem on Tara's skirt, ran a load of laundry through the washer and dryer, baked a batch of brownies. The Burger Barn had closed at eleven, she knew. Was Emily staying late to clean or get ahead on tomorrow's work? Or was she out with Bart Tipton instead? A cold chill crept down Brooke's spine. She was sitting at the kitchen table, trying to concentrate on a book, when she heard the car in the garage.

Emily fumbled with her key at the back door, and tiptoed in. 'I was trying to be quiet,' she said. 'I didn't want to wake you.'

'I was waiting up for you.'

'You didn't need to.' Emily looked exhausted.

'I wanted to. I'm always a little concerned when you're out so late, and alone.' Brooke poured hot water from the kettle into the teapot. 'Would you like a cup?'

'Please.' Emily dropped into a chair. 'Dave and I stayed and talked after closing.'

Relief percolated through Brooke. She waited till the tea had brewed. Then she set a cup in front of Emily, and sat down across from her. 'And what did Dave tell you?' she asked.

Emily sighed. 'That you had all sorts of reasons for refusing to sell that stock, and that I hadn't been fair in not listening to them.'

'That's true,' Brooke said softly.

'And that maybe if Ty starts the company up again, some day my stock will be worth a fortune.'

'What do you think of that?'

'It's a pretty silly attitude. Somebody has to sell him the stock first, or how can the business ever amount to anything? Besides, I need the money money now. Let someone else wait for some day.' Emily sipped her tea, and she looked up fearfully. 'Have you thought about it, Brooke?'

'Yes. And I think Dave has some good points.'

Emily took a breath, as if she was about to plunge into argument again. Then she shook her head and released the breath, as if deciding that it was hopeless to try to convince her sister.

'However, as it happens, I think that this time you're right. Your education is more important right now.'

Emily looked stunned, then she grinned. 'Did you call Ty?'

'I tried, but he's out. But tomorrow morning will do just as well, I'm sure.'

'Brooke, thank you. And I promise, if your stock is worth a million dollars some day, that I'll never, ever complain that I sold out too cheap.'

Brooke laughed. 'You'd better not! Besides, by then you'll be making so much money from your law practice that you'll never miss this.'

'Do you suppose it might be worth something, some day?' asked Emily.

'That stock? I doubt it. I think Ty Marshall is trying to impress Oakley Mills with a gallant gesture—showing everyone what a wonderful person he's become. What's really astonishing is that he knows what a gentleman would do.'

'Come on, Brooke, he's not that bad. I always liked Ty.'

'You were too little when he left to know what he was like.'

'I was thirteen. That's old enough.'

'Not for everything.'

'Well, you seemed to like him well enough back then,' argued Emily.

'Until I found out a few things . . . ' Brooke stared down into her teacup, then raised serious green eyes to her sister's face. 'Emily, I have to ask you about something.'

Emily fidgeted in her chair. 'Don't you mean someone?'

she asked. 'Dave said he'd told you.'

'Yes, as a matter of fact I would like to talk about Bart Tipton.'

'You don't like him, do you?'

'I don't know him very well, Emily. I have to admit that what I know I don't like. You must realise that I prefer it when you bring your friends home, instead of meeting them behind my back.'

'I know.' Emily bit her lip. 'That's why I didn't bring him around—I knew you wouldn't like him. All you needed to hear was his name, and you were against him.'

'Why are you seeing him, Emily? What does Bart Tipton have to offer you?' Brooke's tone was gentle. The last thing she wanted to do was to send Emily screaming up to her room again; the longer they could talk about Bart reasonably, the better the results would be. But it was hard, she thought, picturing the young man as she had seen him last—smoking a cigarette in the library one day, and less than co-operative when she reminded him of the state law against smoking in public places. What Emily saw in him was beyond her.

'Why?' Emily was thoughtful. 'Mainly the fact that you don't like him, I guess, and because you'd tell me that hanging around with Bart wasn't the proper thing for a Carlisle to do. I thought that was silly, you know, because now we're no better than he is.'

Brooke had to smother the urge to throw something at the girl. 'Why? Just because the family money is gone? You say you're not materialistic, Emily—but you seem to think that losing the money made you a different person.'

'Then you explain it to me.'

'It's a thing called character, Emily. The Carlisles have always been leaders in Oakley Mills, people to look up to. That had nothing to do with money——'

'But the cash certainly didn't hurt.' Emily finished her cup of tea.

Brooke watched her thoughtfully. 'You aren't serious about Bart, are you?'

Emily shrugged. She put her cup in the dishwasher. 'No. He's interesting to talk to, but . . . ' She looked up, and the hardness died out of her eyes to be replaced with a shaky smile. 'Wouldn't you rather have me at Cedar than hanging around with Bart here?'

For an instant Brooke couldn't breathe. 'You did it on purpose? You little scamp! You deserve to be locked in your room for that stunt!'

'Please do,' Emily begged. 'Then I could sleep late tomorrow.'

Brooke was suddenly serious. 'Em, you have to quit working so fearfully hard, or you'll get sick. You must have put in thirteen hours at work today, to say nothing of an hour on the tennis court.'

Emily yawned. 'I know. That's a lot of hamburgers. All right. I'm still going to work overtime when I can, but no more double shifts.'

'Good.' Brooke sat there, finishing her tea, after Emily had gone up to bed.

She tried the hotel again, but Tyler still hadn't come in. She wasn't happy with the choice she had made, she decided. She still thought it was a mistake to sell Emily's stock. But it was better than the alternative. If Emily didn't have her chance, heaven only knew what she was capable of doing. Selling was the only answer.

And if it fed Ty Marshall's ego, to believe that he was crushing her pride by buying up pieces of the Carlisle family empire, then so be it, she thought. Emily was far more important than Tyler Marshall would ever be.

Jane was already in the Friends' booth when Brooke reached the library the next morning. 'Look!' she called when she saw Brooke. 'The T-shirts for the carnival prizes came in this morning.' She held up a bright yellow shirt. Printed on the front of it, in three-inch-high letters, was FICTION READERS ARE NOVEL LOVERS.

Brooke winced. 'Who do you think is going to wear that?' she asked.

'You are, for one. All of us who are working in the booths will.'

'Do I have a choice of slogans?'

'Nope. This is the official T-shirt for the first annual library picnic, carnival and ice cream social.'

'The way you keep stringing activities together, Jane, you'll need a billboard at the gate instead of a welcome sign.'

Jane shrugged. 'Wait till you get the receipts, then we'll see if you're laughing. I'm betting we'll make more than a thousand dollars.'

'That would be nice,' Brooke admitted.

'And our goal is to sign up fifty new Friends. But I got a hundred buttons, just in case. Do you think this will do it?' she asked anxiously.

The metal badge had a pin on the back, so it could be fastened to collar or lapel. On the face of it was a drawing of a bookworm, and the slogan, Will you be my FRIEND?

'It's cute,' said Brooke. 'Can I wear a button and skip the T-shirt?'

Jane leered. 'It would increase attendance, that's sure, as soon as the word got out. At a dollar a head for admission, we'd draw every man in town to see you without a shirt!'

'That wasn't quite what I meant.'

'What a shame!' Jane went back to unpacking shirts.

'I didn't know you were working today,' commented Brooke.

'Until the carnival is over, I'll be working every day.'

Brooke smiled at her. 'It's good for you,' she said. 'You'll have to join the real world!'

Speaking of the real world, she reminded herself as she reached her office, she still hadn't managed to catch Ty Marshall. She shut her office door and put a call through to the hotel.

There was still no answer from his room. She left a message at the reception desk, put the telephone down, and sat there for a moment chewing her lower lip. It had been after midnight before she had given up last night; now there was no answer this morning. He hadn't checked out or the hotel clerk would have told her. But in that case, where the heck was he?

And who cares? she asked crossly. Once she had Emily's money—in cash, she reminded herself—Ty Marshall could go straight to the devil. If he hadn't already.

As the day wore on, she became increasingly edgy. She'd skipped lunch and stayed in the building, not wanting to miss him in case he returned her call. She'd done her best to keep a line free, so he could reach her. But there had been no word. Surely he hadn't just ignored her message? He wouldn't have done that, anyway, she thought. He wanted that stock, and he certainly knew that there was nothing else she'd be calling him about.

She was working on next year's budget, and making a hash of the figures, when one of her employees tapped on her door. 'There's a call for you, Miss Carlisle,' she said.

Brooke's pencil went flying. She grabbed the telephone.

'This is Ty Marshall,' the voice at the other end of the line said. She closed her eyes in momentary gratitude.

'Tyler,' she said, forcing her voice to steadiness. 'I'd like to talk to you about the proposition you made last night.'

There was a second of silence. 'I'm afraid I'm too busy for any long discussions at the moment, Brooke.'

So he was going to play hard to get, was he? What did it matter, she thought, if he wanted to exert a little control, and manipulate her a bit? 'It—it wouldn't have to be right now.'

'In that case,' he said, with sudden decision, 'I'll meet you in the cocktail lounge at the hotel at six.'

Two could play that game, she thought. 'Make it ten minutes after. The library doesn't close till six.'

'I'll be waiting,' he said. The telephone clicked in her ear.

Well, she thought. He certainly hadn't acquired a more polished manner in the four years since he'd left Oakley Mills.

The impression was confirmed when she reached the hotel bar. The room was dimly lit, with soft background music and quiet conversations at nearly every table. But there was no Tyler Marshall to be seen.

Reliable, isn't he? she thought sarcastically. It confirmed

the decision she had made, to insist that Emily's stock be paid for in cash. She walked up to the bar. 'Has Mr Marshall been in?' she asked.

The bartender looked her over. 'You're supposed to go up to his room. Suite 500.'

'I beg your pardon?'

'He said there'd be a blonde dish in asking for him. Said to tell you to come up to his room.'

Brooke gritted her teeth. He'd done it on purpose, she knew—inviting her to the bar and then up to his room made her look like a pick-up. Or worse, a call girl . . .

Swallow your pride, she told herself firmly. Sell the stock, get the money, and then you can tear his character apart. It was a certainty that there was plenty she would like to tell him. The question now was whether she could be polite long enough to get Emily's money.

I have to, she thought. I simply have to.

'Suite 500?' she repeated. 'Well, I must admit it's a bit noisy in here to talk business.'

It made her feel a little better, even though she knew the bartender wouldn't believe a word of it.

Suite 500 was a group of rooms on a corner of the old hotel, newly remodelled now, with its turn-of-the-century elegance refurbished. The suite was more like an apartment than a room, she discovered, when Tyler answered the door.

He was coatless, his white shirt-sleeves rolled to the elbow, and in the act of straightening his tie, of dark blue silk with a silvery pattern woven into it. His hair gleamed in the sunlight that fell across the living-room. Just why had it turned prematurely silver? she wondered. Was it still as soft as it had been? She had loved to stroke his hair, to run her fingers through it——Oh, stop acting like a kid with a crush! she told herself crossly.

'I see you got my message,' he said.

'Yes,' Brooke said tightly. She stepped over the threshold, feeling as if a prison door was closing behind her.

'Well,' he said, 'thank you for coming up. What would you like to drink?'

'Whatever you have. I really don't want anything, Tyler, except a couple of minutes of your time. It shouldn't take long.'

'Sit down,' he said. It was not a request.

She settled herself gingerly on the edge of the couch. Across the room, she could see through the half-open bedroom door. Ty had come up in the world, she thought. It looked as if he had learned to enjoy his money. Suites and silk neckties—the old Ty would have been clumsy and shy in a setting like this, she thought. This Tyler knew his way around.

He set a Martini glass in front of her. She looked at it warily, and then up at him.

Ty sat down beside her and sipped his Martini. 'Go ahead,' he invited. 'There's nothing wrong with the drink. I don't drug ladies—at least not the ones who come to my room willingly.'

Brooke bit her lip. 'I wouldn't exactly say I was here of my own free choice,' she pointed out. But she picked up the drink. It was good, she decided. Just dry enough.

He leaned back, and studied her over the rim of his glass. Then he started to laugh. It was low, throaty, musical. It would have been an infectious laugh, if Brooke had seen anything funny in the whole situation.

She stood it as long as she could. Finally she said, 'May I share the joke?'

'It just struck me that you're hardly my idea of a librarian, Brooke. Look at you, sitting in a man's hotel room, with your hair down, sipping an intoxicating beverage——'

'You, Tyler, are hardly my idea of a gentleman.'

'Yes, I know,' he said pleasantly. 'You've made that very clear in the past.' His eyes were pale grey and cool; he seemed to be taking an inventory of her as he gazed at her intently. 'On the other hand,' he added thoughtfully, 'you aren't married. That does fit my picture of——'

'I'm not precisely over the hill,' Brooke snapped.

'Why aren't you married? I'm sure there've been plenty of men hanging around. There was certainly no shortage when I left town. Tell me, Brooke, didn't any of them come up to your standards?'

'Don't flatter yourself that you're the reason I'm still single, Tyler.'

'Or didn't your new behaviour measure up to their standards?' he added smoothly. Before she had a chance to gasp at the blithe insult, he added, 'You used to call me Ty.'

'Look, I didn't come here to argue.'

He raised a quizzical eyebrow. 'I hadn't noticed that we were arguing. But if you'd like to begin——'

'I came here to talk business.'

Tyler gestured with his glass. 'Then by all means, talk.'

'You told me yesterday that you wanted to buy our stock,' she said, keeping her composure with an effort. She took another small sip of the Martini, and set it aside. 'Tara's shares and mine are not for sale. But Emily's fifteen per cent is.'

He didn't seem to hear. 'Don't you like your Martini?' he asked. He sounded very concerned.

'It's fine. Didn't you hear me, Tyler? I said I came to sell you Emily's stock.'

'I heard.' He seemed unconcerned. 'Are you sure you wouldn't prefer something else to drink? Martinis aren't everyone's favourite, I know.'

'I would prefer to talk business. Frankly, I think the shares are worth more than thirty dollars.'

For a moment she thought he wasn't going to answer at all. 'At one time, they were worth ten times that,' he said at last. 'If you can get that much, I'd advise you to sell in a hurry.'

She hadn't expected that it would bother him. It was only an idle threat, after all—who else would be crazy enough to buy the stock of a defunct company? 'I'm sure Alison didn't sell for a mere thirty dollars a share,' she said demurely.

'You're quite right.'

Brooke reached for her Martini glass. 'Well, I won't sell for less than Alison got,' she said firmly. She sounded sullen, she knew. She didn't care, as long as it got her what she wanted. She was determined to drive the best bargain she could, for Emily's sake. She certainly didn't care what he thought of her.

Ty didn't react at all for a few seconds. Then he turned his head to look at her, and the sunlight sparkled off his silver hair. 'Won't you?' he said, very softly. A slow smile spread across his mouth, and his white teeth gleamed. 'Are you certain you want to agree to the same terms?' he asked. 'Alison had some . . . unique ideas.'

You put your foot in that one, Brooke, she told herself. She should have expected something like that. Had he married Alison, after all? She glanced at his hand, trying to be carefully casual. No ring there. But of course that didn't mean much. He had told her once that he could never wear a ring, because the machinery he worked with made it too dangerous. It was true enough; many a man had lost a finger when his wedding ring became caught in a machine. But had it only been a convenient excuse for Ty?

'I'm talking money,' she said firmly. 'Unlike Alison, I'm not interested in anything else you might have to offer.'

'Of course you aren't,' he agreed. 'You made that perfectly clear long ago, didn't you?' His voice was silky.

'Our broken engagement has nothing to do with now,' she said, uneasily. 'And it has nothing to do with Emily's stock.'

'Have you changed since then, Brooke? The last time I kissed you, you played the offended virgin. Is that why you haven't found a man to your liking?' Very slowly, very deliberately, he took the glass from her and set it on the coffee-table. His hand was warm against the back of her neck. 'Or do you even remember how it used to be? Shall I remind you?'

She stifled a shiver as he drew her closer. He was out to exact his price, she thought, his revenge for the injury she had done to his pride. Once they had made a deal, she wouldn't be seeing him again; he knew that as well as she did. What difference did it make if he kissed her first? It wasn't important. She would put up with it as the price

of Emily's education. After all, he had kissed her before
and she had survived. She would show him that he no
longer had that kind of power over her.

His mouth closed warmly over hers, gentle, knowing.
On that long-ago summer afternoon he had demanded a
response, and her frightened body had denied it. Now, he
neither arrogantly demanded nor humbly begged—it was
as if he simply expected, because he was a man and she a
woman, that she would respond to him.

I'll play along, Brooke thought muzzily. If I can just
make him think he's defeated me . . .

He kissed her as if that afternoon in the garden had
never been. Her lips relaxed under the pressure of his,
and his tongue explored her mouth, unhurriedly. She
could taste the gin. She closed her eyes; her breath came
unevenly. She had forgotten, she thought, how the sensa-
tions could build, one on top of another, until she wanted
to cling to him, to beg him not to stop kissing her ever
again . . .

'You tempt me, Brooke,' he muttered, against her lips.
'You really do. I'd like to see just how far you'd go to
get what you want.'

She stiffened in his arms, suddenly afraid of him.

'But I'm an ethical man,' he went on, very softly. He
was breathing a little unsteadily too, she thought.

His fingertips were caressing her temple, brushing the
soft blonde hair back from her face. She wanted to tear
herself away from him, but the pressure of his fingers was
almost hypnotic.

'It wouldn't be honest not to tell you that I don't want
to buy your stock now at any price.'

For an instant, she thought she had imagined the
words. Then, as she realised that he had really said it,
returning reason pulled her away from him, abruptly, and
she sat up straight and tense on the edge of the couch.

Ty looked her over carefully, without hurry. 'No,' he
said, 'you haven't changed a bit, have you, Brooke? Sweet
and willing when it's to your advantage, and cold and
hard otherwise.' His hand slid casually down her arm. It

was an intimate, possessive gesture. His touch sent shivers through her whole body.

She pulled away from him and stalked across the room to the windows. Oh, he'd really made a fool of her this time, that was sure, she told herself wearily. The worst part was that he was right; she had been prepared to let him kiss her—maybe even more than that—so long as she got what she wanted. But what did it matter? Let him exact his price.

'Thirty dollars a share,' she said. 'Two hundred and fifty shares. Seven thousand, five hundred in cash——'

'You won't get it from me,' he interrupted. 'I told you at the club yesterday that I'd made my final offer, and if you were interested to call me. You told me not to wait around to hear from you. I did, though. When I hadn't gotten an answer by the time I went out to dinner last night, I went ahead with alternative arrangements. I already own a majority of the stock, Brooke. I don't need Emily's shares.'

'Oh, my God,' she whispered. 'You can't do this——'

'Why can't I?' he asked reasonably. 'All I wanted was control. I have it. Why should I tie up more capital to get complete ownership?'

'But you offered me a deal! And I tried to call you last night. I tried till almost midnight——'

'I did warn you that I'd be going out,' he said. He had arranged himself comfortably on the couch, his feet stretched out under the coffee-table.

Brooke licked her dry lips. 'Alternative arrangements, you said?' she muttered. 'What did you do?'

'Use your head, Brooke. I bought out the other partners, that's what. Between Alison's shares and what the other two held, I now have fifty-five per cent. Sorry, my dear. You had your chance.'

He looked far from sorry, she thought. He looked delighted.

'What am I supposed to tell Emily?' she whispered.

Tyler shrugged. 'The truth might be nice,' he said. 'I certainly don't have anything against Emily. I'd hate for her to get the idea that I did.'

'But she was counting on that money.'

'I'm sure I can't be expected to feel guilty about that,' he pointed out. 'You did, after all, tell me last night that you were doing extremely well and didn't need my money.'

Her arms were crossed tightly, as if she were hugging herself. She stared out across the court-house square and noted, half-consciously, that from this window he could see the library. He'd probably stood there and watched her walk across to meet him, and gloated about what he had planned for her . . .

I will not beg, she told herself, and gritted her teeth. That's what he wants—he'd like to have me throw myself at his feet and plead with him. But I will not give him the satisfaction.

She turned from the window. 'In that case,' she said, trying to keep her voice from trembling, 'I suppose I should wish you all the best of luck in your new venture. Especially since any increase in the company's value will mean that Tara and Emily and I will benefit—we'll get almost half of the dividends.'

He was smiling 'I don't thing that I've ever said anything about my plans for Carlisle Products,' he said gently.

'You're not going to reopen the plant?' There was a catch in her voice, which disgusted her. What difference did it make to her? If Tyler wanted to paper a wall with the stock certificates, she didn't care.

'Let's just say that at the moment I'm keeping my options open. Can I buy you dinner—partner?'

Her spine straightened. 'No, thanks, Tyler. I don't want to be seen with you.' It was a dirty thing to say, and the instant the words were out she regretted it.

He was smiling grimly, but there was no sparkle of humour in his eyes. 'Let me remind you, madam librarian, that you are in my room—and in my power at the moment.'

'So what are you going to do?' she jibed. 'Tell the whole town that I came here to sleep with you?'

'And didn't get to the bedroom,' he agreed. 'But only because I didn't push you. You were prepared to sleep with me, weren't you, Brooke? What a shame for you, my dear, that I can see through your motives just as easily as—with the sunshine coming through that window behind you—I can see through that dress.'

She jumped and stepped aside, out of the stream of sunlight.

He was laughing. 'Don't be ashamed,' he said. 'It's still a very nice shape, after all.'

She would have demolished him, then, told him what a rotten excuse for a man he was, but her throat was so tight that the words would not come out. Instead, she walked across the room as regally as she could manage, painfully aware of his appraising eyes, and slammed the door behind her.

She wanted to lean against the wall in the elevator and cry, but she was damned if she'd show such weakness. Instead, she held her head high as she walked back across the square, wondering if he was standing in the window of Suite 500, watching her.

Not until she turned the car into the drive at Oakley did the tears come, and even then she forced them back because Tara was playing in the kitchen.

The child came running. 'Emily went on to work,' she said.

'That's a relief,' muttered Brooke.

'I'm having a tea party for my dolls,' Tara confided.

'That sounds lovely, darling. What would you like for dinner?'

'I was hungry, so I already ate.'

I know I should ask what she had, Brooke thought. Tara's idea of a balanced meal would horrify a dietitian, and the very idea that no one had been at home to supervise what the child ate—I should be ashamed of myself, she thought, but tonight I'm just too tired to care. If she ate pickles and chocolate cake for supper tonight, it isn't going to kill her.

'I'm going up to my room to lie down for a little while,' she said.

Tara was already reabsorbed in her dolls. 'We'll be very, very quiet,' she promised.

'Thank you, darling.' And thank heaven that Emily wasn't at home. To explain to her, right now, that she would have to manage college without the bonanza from her stock was more than Brooke could face at the moment.

And why? she asked herself fiercely. He had wanted that stock yesterday. He had offered far more than it was worth. And now, today, he didn't want it at all.

She closed the door of the big master bedroom with a sigh of relief, kicked off her shoes, and flung herself down on the bed. This was her sanctuary; redecorating it had been her one luxury in the last year. Now it was a flower garden in yellow and white and green. It was a cool, crisp, refreshing room, a place that restored her faith and her courage. But not today.

What had caused Tyler's change of plan? Had he really bought out the other two partners? Or had he just been toying with her yesterday?

You did it, Brooke, she told herself. You are responsible. You called him nasty names, and were abrupt and rude, and treated him like dirt. It was no wonder that he had changed his mind, and decided instead to carry through that long-ago threat to destroy her pride, to humiliate her.

He'd done a pretty thorough job of that, she thought reluctantly. She was too embarrassed even to blush, as she thought of the way he had kissed her. And she hadn't protested, she had just relaxed in his arms and allowed him to touch her, to caress her, as if he had the right.

And how much more would she have allowed, she wondered, and sat up abruptly, her body tense. Obviously, he believed that if he hadn't broken it off, she'd have ended up in his bed.

'Never!' she said. It was a tight, harsh exclamation. Not for anything would she do that—not even for Emily. And certainly not with Ty Marshall. The very idea of that man putting his hands on her made her skin crawl.

And yet she had allowed him to hold her. The brush of his fingers on her skin had been like liquid fire, and when he had kissed her, part of her had not wanted him to stop.

'This is ridiculous,' she told herself violently. 'Stop this nonsense and think about something else.'

Oh, God, she thought. How am I going to tell Emily what I've done?

CHAPTER FOUR

MAYBE I just won't tell Emily, Brooke decided. There had to be another way to get the money. Emily certainly didn't care where it came from, just as long as she could enrol at Cedar College this fall.

But surely she had the right to know? Brooke felt like a traitor.

'You're a yellow, cowardly, chicken-hearted traitor,' she told herself. Then she rehearsed her story in front of her dressing-table mirror, fixed a firm smile on her face, and went downstairs to wait for Emily.

She helped Tara with her arithmetic homework and then hurried the child through her bath and off to bed. Just in case Emily was early tonight, she wanted to make sure Tara wouldn't hear the discussion.

When Brooke went to tuck her in, Tara was already snuggled up under a light blanket, her favourite doll on one side, her battered teddy bear on the other, patting back a yawn.

'Goodnight, Tara,' said Brooke, just as she always did. 'Darling, dream the night away, and wake to another lovely day . . . ' It was the little litany that she remembered from her childhood, just as her mother had always said it to Brooke when she came to kiss her goodnight. It was foolish, perhaps, to put so much emphasis on a silly rhyme, but if saying it made her feel better, what did it matter?

'I have a question,' Tara announced. 'Why do you always say it'll be a lovely day tomorrow? 'Cause sometimes it isn't, you know. It rains, or it snows——'

'But it's always a lovely day, because it's new and fresh, and we can leave all our old troubles behind and start over.' It's a beautiful philosophy, Brooke thought. Now if I can just put it into practice!

Tara looked puzzled. 'Will you have a lovely day tomorrow?' she asked. 'You look awfully unhappy tonight.'

Oh, no, Brooke thought. It's bad enough to deal with eagle-eyed Emily, but if Tara's going to start reading my mind, I might as well just give up. 'I don't know, Tara. But it will start out fresh and clean, I'm sure of that.'

'I don't like it when you're unhappy,' Tara confided. Then she snuggled down into her pillow.

And that, Brooke told herself, is that. She remembered abruptly that she'd had no dinner, and went down to search the refrigerator. Just what had Tara eaten? she wondered, and felt guilty all over again before she reminded herself that it really hadn't been her fault. If it hadn't been for Ty, she would have been home on time.

Damn Ty Marshall anyway, she thought. He'd been playing games with her! He'd known what she wanted as soon as he had received her message, but instead of coming straight out and telling her that he was no longer interested, he'd played with her as he might a fish who'd taken the bait, first letting her run, then patiently reeling her in.

It wasn't a very pleasant image, and she stood there for a long time, staring unseeingly at her glass of milk. Had Ty cut the line and let her go? Or was he simply letting her run again, thinking for a while that she was free?

The telephone rang. 'Hi,' said Emily. 'I was checking to see if you'd gotten home yet.'

'I was just a bit late, and I didn't have chance to call.'

'Sorry about leaving Tara alone like that, but I didn't know what else to do.'

'She was fine. Emily——'

'Did you talk to Ty?'

Brooke drew a deep breath, and prepared herself to launch into her story. I reconsidered, she was going to say, and borrowed against the value of the stock rather than selling it. But the words wouldn't come out right. 'I talked to him,' she said finally.

'Good.' Emily's sigh of relief was clear. 'I'm glad to
have that out of the way. Is it all right with you if I go
to the late show at the drive-in theatre? A bunch of the
kids will be there, and Dave said I could leave a little
early.'

'Who's going?' asked Brooke.

'The whole gang. Kris will bring me home, and Dave's
going to lock my bike inside the Burger Barn tonight.
You won't even have to wait up to be sure your darling
gets home safe and sound.'

And that way I won't have to tell you about Tyler
tonight, Brooke thought. I really am a first-class chicken,
she accused herself, a little ashamed of the relief she felt.
But at least it would give her a chance to think about her
options. 'Sure, Emily. I'll see you in the morning.'

But morning shed no further light on the matter, only
increasing Brooke's determination not to tell Emily the
whole story until she had an answer worked out.

Brooke came back from her early walk through the
woods feeling a little better. On a morning as beautiful as
this, with the cool, crisp air, the fresh pale green of the
leaves, and the bluebells beginning to flower, surely nothing
could be as bad as it had looked last night.

Today would be a new, fresh start, she had told Tara
last night. Perhaps it would be exactly that, she thought.
She'd go and see Ben Adams at the bank this morning,
and see about taking out a loan against Emily's stock
certificates. Ben had been one of Elliot's two partners in
Carlisle Products; if Ty had been telling the truth last
night, Ben had sold his shares so he knew what they were
worth. It would probably work out better that way,
anyway, she told herself. Emily would have the money
she needed, and she'd still have the stock. Perhaps in a
few years she could sell it, pay back the loan, and still
have a little left over . . .

It sounded good, she told herself. She hoped Ben
Adams would agree.

Emily was whistling in the kitchen as Brooke came in.
She had just pulled a pan of muffins out of the oven.
'Blueberry,' she said, waving one in Brooke's direction.

'You're ambitious for this hour. What time did you get home last night?'

Emily grinned. 'It wasn't last night, exactly,' she evaded. 'It was more like early this morning.'

'Youth,' Brooke sighed wearily. 'How you can do it . . .'

'You're not exactly ancient, you know, so stop mourning about your loss.' Emily put a muffin on Tara's plate. 'Don't burn yourself, Tara the Terrible.'

Brooke cut a muffin in half and watched butter melt into it. 'Emily, did I ever tell you why Mom chose Tara's name?'

'No. Why?'

Even Tara looked intrigued, though not enough to ignore her breakfast.

'Because she didn't think it could be shortened into a nickname. She was tired of hearing you called Emmy.'

Emily put her muffin pan in the sink to soak. 'So? I didn't shorten Tara's name. I merely added an appropriate adjective.'

Brooke sighed. 'Obviously, Mom had no idea of your potential, Emily Carlisle.'

'I know,' Emily grinned. 'It was her misfortune not to be better acquainted with me. So tell me about yesterday. Did Ty jump at the chance to buy the stock? When do I get my money?'

'What's the hurry?' Brooke evaded. 'School won't start for three months.'

'It might as well be in the bank, earning a few dollars in interest.'

'I'll deposit it in your account.' Just as soon as I figure out where it's coming from, she thought.

'I'll need some of it in a couple of weeks. I want to go to orientation, of course. And they're having a tennis camp then, too, for the people who got scholarships.'

Brooke swallowed hard and glanced at the clock. 'All right, Emily. Come on, Tara, finish that muffin and off to school with you.'

Tara stuck her bottom lip out. 'Eight more days till summer vacation,' she mourned. 'Can I at least go swimming at the club this afternoon?'

'I can keep an eye on her,' offered Emily. 'I have a tennis lesson anyway.'

What a change in Emily's attitude the whole thing had made, Brooke thought. It was as though a different girl had moved in; with her hopes restored, Emily was gentler somehow, and sweeter. It squashed Brooke's last lingering hope that perhaps, if the loan fell through, Emily could be persuaded to settle for a year of junior college after all.

She kissed Tara goodbye and started to clean up the mess in the kitchen. It seemed a never-ending battle. Mrs Wilson never had this much trouble keeping the house in order, she thought, and regretted the day that she had had to cut the housekeeper's salary out of her budget.

Ben Adams's Cadillac was parked outside the bank's front door and he was standing on the step, his key in his hand when Brooke drove by. She made an illegal U-turn and pulled in beside his car.

He looked up. 'Hello, Brooke.' He looked a little wary, she thought, as if he might be ashamed of himself, or concerned about what she might say.

'I know you're not open for business yet, Ben,' she said, 'but I need to talk to you for a minute before I go to work.'

He shrugged. 'Sure. Come on in.'

He made a quick check of the building and then ushered her into his office. He leaned back in his big leather chair and said, 'Well, Brooke, what can I do for you?'

'I understand Ty Marshall bought your Carlisle stock, Ben.'

'I wasn't trying to keep it a secret, Brooke.' His voice was gruff. 'I'm sorry if you're displeased, but business is business.'

'And what about George? Did he sell out too?'

'Sure he did. The price was fair.'

So Tyler hadn't been stretching the truth last night, she thought. With Alison's shares, he really did hold the majority of the stock.

'I understand he made an offer on your shares too, Brooke.'

'That's right.' She took a deep breath. 'Ben, I don't want to sell that stock. But Emily needs money for school this autumn. I'd like to borrow against her shares, as her guardian.'

'What have you got in mind?' he asked.

'Five thousand or so. It's worth far more than that . . .'

'Says who?' The banker's voice was matter-of-fact. 'Until Ty Marshall came back to town, those stock certificates were about as much good as yesterday's newspaper.'

'Look, I don't know what he paid you, Ben, but he offered me thirty dollars a share.'

Ben Adams's eyebrows went up almost into his hair. He must have sold for less, Brooke thought, and cursed her own stubbornness. 'I don't want to borrow that much . . .'

'I'd take him up on it, Brook. Nobody's going to make you a better offer than Ty will.'

She didn't dare admit to him that Ty no longer wanted it. 'I don't want to give up the stock, Ben. Don't you see that?' It wasn't a lie, she told herself. She was just selecting the portions of the truth she wanted to tell.

'Yes, I see it, but I think it's damned short-sighted of you.'

There was a long silence. 'Do you mean that you don't want to make the loan?'

The leather chair creaked as Ben pulled himself up to his desk. 'What I want to do doesn't come into it, Brooke. I'd loan you the money in a minute if it was up to me. I trust you to repay it. But I can't take the stock as collateral. As far as the bank is concerned, it's worthless.'

'But it does have value, Ben! When Tyler reopens that plant——'

'Is he going to?' Ben's voice was low.

Brooke was silent for a long moment. 'I don't know,' she admitted.

'That, my dear, makes two of us. Ty Marshall never

was a chatterbox, and these days he's saying even less than he used to.'

'But why would he buy it if he's not planning to manufacture something there?'

Ben shrugged. 'A tax write-off, maybe. Who knows?'

'All right,' she said. 'Let's stop speculating about Ty's plans. You just told me that you trust me. Make me a personal loan—whatever terms you like.'

'Using what as security? Frankly, Brooke, in every way but character you're not too good a risk. You're young and single—not what a bank defines as exactly stable. You've got a decent job, but you'll never get rich as a librarian. You have two dependants, and a terrific amount of overhead expense as long as you insist on keeping Oakley Manor. Even your car still has a loan against it.'

It was unanswerable. It was also true.

'I'd trust you, Brooke; there's no question in my mind that you'd pay it back, even if you had to scrimp on food to do it. But my board of directors would have my head for making unsecured loans like that.'

'The stock is all I have to offer you.'

'Well, there it is.' Ben sighed and went on in a softer tone. 'Send Emily in and I'll talk to her about some of the special loan programmes for students. We might be able to work something out, and then it would be her responsibility, not yours, to pay it back after she graduates.'

But then I'd have to tell her about Ty, Brooke thought. She shook her head.

Ben misinterpreted her concern. 'You have enough to handle right now, my dear,' he said gently. 'It's time for Emily to start shouldering the responsibility for her own problems. It's not unfair to her—you'd be expecting no more of her than your father asked of you. One hell of a lot less, if fact.'

'I already had my education,' Brooke pointed out.

'I know—but you've taken on a big job with Emily and Tara. Reconsider, Brooke. Sell Ty the darned stock. Let him see what he can do with it.'

I wish I still had that choice, she thought.

Ben saw the tightness in her face. 'You're a stubborn girl,' he sighed, and Brooke didn't bother to correct him. 'You're Elliot's daughter, that's for sure. Just as hard-headed as he was.'

Brooke picked up her handbag. 'If Ty does start the company up again,' she observed, 'Emily's share could be worth almost a hundred thousand dollars, just as it was before the crash came.'

'You don't need to remind me of what it used to be worth,' Ben said drily. 'Remember? I got burned on Carlisle stock myself.'

'It could be worth even more than that,' murmured Brooke. It was a grudging admission of respect for Tyler's business ability.

'That's right,' Ben agreed smoothly. 'And the day Carlisle Products turns a profit again, you bring those certificates in and I'll be happy to make you a loan. You'll notice I'm not holding my breath. In the meantime, those shares are worth precisely what Ty Marshall says they're worth—and then only to him, because nobody else is going to be fool enough to buy them.'

And that, thought Brooke, was the end of that. Another door had closed in her face.

'You're pretty glum tonight,' observed Dave.

Brooke looked away from the golf tournament that was featured on the big television set in the club lounge. She force a smile. It wasn't often that she and Dave had an evening out together; she should be enjoying it instead of fretting about that conversation with Ben Adams this morning. 'Don't you feel disloyal?' she asked, gesturing at the tenderloin sandwich he was consuming.

'Not in the least. Just because I manage fast-food places doesn't mean I eat there all the time.' He looked around, and then leaned across the table to whisper conspiratorially, 'Just between you and me, after a while you begin to think you're eating the same hamburger day after day.'

Brooke laughed.

Dave's face cleared. 'Well, that's better,' he said. 'I was beginning to think that you'd sworn off smiling altogether.'

'No. It's just that—well, I'm having problems with Emily again.'

'Not Bart Tipton? I knew I should have beaten that kid up!'

'Oh, no. We've got that all settled.' She debated about confessing the whole thing—Tyler, the stock, her attempt to get a loan, No, she thought. If Dave even found out that she had gone to Ty's hotel room, he'd be unhappy. Not that he really had any right to complain, as he might if she was wearing his ring—but they did have a sort of understanding. She wouldn't blame him for being upset.

'Frankly,' said Dave, 'sometimes I think somebody ought to spank Emily. She's a good kid, but you could put her common sense on the head of a pin.'

That goes for me too, Brooke thought. Anyone with intelligence would have grabbed Ty Marshall's money and run. But no—Brooke had wanted revenge. Well, revenge would have tasted much sweeter if she had been able to afford the price. It was stupid to let something that happened years ago still bother her so much. It was over, and she should be thankful she hadn't been married to him.

'Don't look now,' said Dave, 'but your friend Marshall just came in off the golf course.'

'That's all I need,' muttered Brooke.

'I wonder if he's planning to move here permanently.'

'I presume so, since he's joining the club.' And why would he have done that, she wondered, if he wasn't planning to reopen the Carlisle plant? She wondered if Ben Adams knew that Ty had applied for membership.

'I hadn't come to town yet when he left,' Dave reminded her. 'So tell me, what's so special about Tyler Marshall? From what everybody says, he was nothing grand when he left here—just an assistant at the plant. So why is everyone bowing and scraping and speaking in whispers around him now?'

'I hadn't noticed that anyone was.'

'They certainly all listen to what he says.'

'Oh. That's a different matter altogether. You see, Ty is that unusual animal—the honest-to-goodness self-made millionaire. At least I imagine that he must be by now. After he left here, he invented a new twist that revolutionised the manufacture of typewriter ribbons, thereby making every existing company obsolete. You must have heard people talking about it.'

Dave shook his head. 'Maybe they were talking—but I apparently wasn't listening.'

'For every ribbon made today, the manufacturer pays Ty for the privilege of using his idea. People around here are awed by Tyler's success. But awe isn't the same as respect. Awe wears off. Mere money doesn't buy social position, you see.'

Brooke hadn't been listening to the normal buzz of conversation around her, and so she hadn't noticed when the room fell silent as attention turned to a critical putt on the television screen. It wasn't until the words had been uttered that she realised her voice had been clearly audible across the room.

Heads turned across the lounge. Only Tyler himself seemed not to have heard. He was holding a Martini. He took a sip, set it down, and beckoned to a waitress.

In for a penny, in for a pound thought Brooke. One thing was certain: it was too late to back out now. Besides, she wanted to injure him, to strike out at this man who had so casually made a fool of her, and enjoyed doing it. He had played games with her. Well, it was time someone challenged him.

'Good breeding is what really matters,' she added clearly. 'And family background. Those things can't be purchased, only earned over time.' She glanced at Tyler, then turned back to Dave.

'Brooke!' he breathed, horrified.

'In some cases, of course,' she finished, 'it would take a great deal of time.'

The waitress set a cocktail napkin in front of Brooke, and put a Martini glass on it. 'Mr Marshall's compliments,' she said.

'I wouldn't drink it, Brooke,' Dave advised. 'He probably had them spike it with cyanide.'

She glanced over at Tyler. He raised his matching glass in a silent toast and smiled.

She had to admit that he had acquired a bit of class, somewhere along the line. The old Ty Marshall would have been fiercely angry at that attack.

And perhaps the new one is too, she told herself, but has just learned to hide it better. From somewhere in the back of her mind, the scent of gladioli, crushed into a scarlet paste on a dusty path, rose to haunt her. She tried to suppress a shiver, and pushed the glass aside.

'Honestly, Brooke,' hissed Dave, 'you don't have any more sense than Emily does!'

'Thanks,' she returned. 'I'm glad you have such a high opinion of us both.'

'It's true,' he said. 'It was over between you years ago. So why set out to alienate the man?'

She was beginning to feel a little ashamed of herself. What had happened to her resolution to let the past die away?

'Anyway, that whole business about social position is nonsense, Brooke, and you know it. Nobody takes that stuff seriously any more.'

'I've been told that the Carlisles aren't any better than else,' she said clearly. 'Very recently—by Emily. Perhaps you two have more in common than you realised!'

'It amazes me that she has that much sense. To be honest, Brooke, you haven't been the best example for her, pretending that losing the business didn't make any difference in your lives.'

'And I suppose you're an expert?' she asked politely.

'No, but I do know that you aren't doing Emily any favour by letting her think she might still get her expensive education. The junior college here, or the state university, would be much more sensible, under the circumstances.'

'Oh?' she said. 'Is that why you counselled her not to cash in her stock?'

'What good would it do? It wouldn't even get her through the first year. I'm certainly not going to help support Emily's education if she insists on going to Cedar College.'

Brooke was coldly furious. 'No one has ever asked you to.'

'Well, it's been plainly understood—'

'Has it?'

'We have talked about getting married some day.' His eyes were sad, as if he regretted bringing the subject up. 'I always assumed I'd help with your sisters. But I must admit to having some doubts about your judgement lately.'

'I'm sure you plan to expound on that statement,' Brooke said sweetly.

'For one thing, you just keep pouring money into that house, when if you had any sense you'd sell the thing——'

'And let it be cut up into shabby little apartments? Not Oakley Manor! Mother left it to me because she knew I'd take care of it.'

He sighed with exasperation. 'That was a different age, Brooke. Your mother expected you'd have plenty of money. She wouldn't expect you to impoverish yourself to keep that house up.'

'Look, Dave——'

'We could sell it and buy a nice small house.'

'I don't want another house. Oakley is my home.'

'That's exactly the attitude I'm talking about,' he said. 'You're stubborn, Brooke. You're throwing money away, month after month, as if you didn't have a care in the world——'

'You never told me you expected me to sell Oakley.'

'I know. I just assumed that once you got over the shock of your father's death, you'd do the sensible thing.'

'I appreciate your concern, but Oakley is my home. And it is my money I'm spending.'

'That's right,' he agreed. 'One thing we all know is that I can't afford the upkeep on Oakley. Neither can you, but you'll never admit it.'

She thought that one over, looking for hidden meanings. 'Does that mean you wouldn't be willing to live there?' she asked.

'I think we'd better go,' said Dave. He scrawled his name across the bill and stood up.

They walked out to the parking lot in silence. Then Brooke said, 'I'm not ready to let this drop, Dave.'

He sighed. 'All right. We'd have to come to some agreement about Oakley, that's for sure, before there's any discussion of getting married.'

'And your definition of an agreement is to sell it and buy a tract house.'

'It's the only thing that makes sense, Brooke.' The car started off with a jerk. 'The only thing that wouldn't strap us financially.'

'And in this smaller house,' she asked, 'would there be room for Emily and Tara? Or am I supposed to desert them, just as you want me to leave Oakley? You must admit it puts a damper on romance to have a nine-year-old around all the time.'

'Oh, come on, Brooke! Stop twisting my words. I never asked you to dump Emily and Tara—just to be realistic about money. It's not a crime to sell a house, for heaven's sake!'

'I will not sell Oakley.'

'And I will not mortgage my future to keep a roof on the damned thing!'

The silence in the car was like a curtain. Dave tried to break it. 'Brooke,' he said, 'we've both said a lot of things tonight that we'll regret. Let's just drop it, and talk about it this weekend, all right?'

'I'm not sure there's anything left to talk about. You've made your feelings very plain.'

'Dammit, Brooke! There's one thing I haven't said, and it's as true as any of the others. I love you. But I'm scared to marry you. You don't have the Carlisle money any more, and unless you scale down your expectations, I don't think I can afford you.'

That was patently unfair, she thought. She had cut every corner she could. Keeping Oakley was her only luxury. And she was managing it now, by herself. Surely if they were married, there would be no problem?

'I'm doing fine, Dave! And with both of us working, we could——'

'Keep Oakley and send Emily off to Cedar College? I'm afraid not. Do you realise what kind of money we're talking about?'

'The Carlisles are a package deal, Dave.'

'I know that, and I accept it. I may not like it, but I'll put up with it. I'm just not sure that you and I could ever agree on what should be done for Emily and Tara.'

'The truth is,' Brooke challenged, 'you don't want to be responsible for anyone except Dave Sheridan.'

'I have to admit that taking on a ready-made family isn't my idea of heaven. If I'm going to raise kids, I'd rather they were my own. Your sisters are terrific, but—well, I can't help thinking of how nice it would be if it was just the two of us.'

'At least you're honest about it.' So much for the charming prince of the fairy story, she thought, who loved the princess so much that he gladly took on her family's woes . . .

'I want to do things for myself too, Brooke. We'd be financially strapped for fifteen years, just for college bills. I don't want to live that way.'

'Then I guess you'd better run while you have the chance,' she said softly.

'To say nothing of this—this white elephant!' Dave stopped the car at the end of Oakley's drive, and the headlights reflected in a million facets from the diamond-paned windows of the long living-room and the study. 'If you'd only sell it and buy a smaller house, maybe we could manage the rest. Not Cedar, though—I just don't see how we could make that work.'

I thought I knew him, she reflected sadly. I thought Dave was the kind of guy who would help to shoulder the responsibility. I thought he gave Emily that job because he liked her and wanted to help her. And I thought he really cared about Tara. I never suspected that he was putting on a front to impress me.

She could have Dave, she knew, if she was willing to wash her hands of Emily's dreams. Tara—well, he'd come around to accepting Tara. She was only a child, and Dave wasn't unrealistic enough to expect her to put Tara into an orphanage or foster-home.

She looked up at Oakley Manor, gleaming under the light of a full moon. It would break her heart to give it up. But Dave didn't consider that. He had only looked at the dollars and cents, not the human emotion. She had never thought he was inflexible about money, just that he was careful.

'This white elephant, as you so charmingly refer to it,' she said firmly, 'is my home. And I do not plan to give it up.'

'You'd prefer to mortgage our future?'

'Dave, I don't think we have a future. Not together.'

There was a long silence. At the back door, he said, 'So you're choosing Oakley, and your unrealistic hopes for your sisters, over me?'

'I don't see that I have a choice,' said Brooke, and her voice shook just a little. 'My mother asked me to take care of Oakley. My father asked me to do my best for Tara and Emily. They need me, Dave.'

'So you're turning your back on what you want?'

'But you see, Dave, this is what I want. I thought I could have all that, and you too. But you've made me see that it wouldn't work. We'd be fighting a dozen times a day, and whoever lost the battle would resent the winner. We have no place to compromise.'

'We'll talk about it this weekend.'

Would it change anything? He might give in for the moment, she thought, and agree to keep Oakley. He might even agree to let Emily have a try at Cedar College. But the battles would only be beginning: every time there was a shortage of cash, they would go through it all again.

'If you insist,' she said, 'we can talk about it again. But I doubt we'll reach any different conclusion. Goodnight, Dave. I thank you for being honest with me.'

He kicked at a loose pebble on the sidewalk. 'You know, that's part of why I love you,' he said, as if it confused him just a little. 'That damned Carlisle pride.'

The phrase echoed uncomfortably in her memory.

'That's unfortunate for you,' she agreed.

'Yeah,' he said. 'Because it's the same thing that would make it impossible to live with you.'

'Goodnight, Dave,' she said. She reached up and kissed his cheek, lightly, as she would have kissed a brother, her fingertips cool against his face. Then she went inside, closed the door behind her, and leaned against it.

'Well,' said Emily. 'Aren't you the sly one?'

She was washing dishes. Tara was up on a kitchen stool, industriously pressing a cookie cutter into a circle of chocolate dough. The scene was so incredibly warm and homely that Brooke just wanted to throw her arms out and embrace the girls, the room, the whole world.

'Did Dave take his comeuppance well?' asked Emily.

Brooke blinked. 'What on earth makes you think——Were you eavesdropping?'

Emily laughed. 'So you did tell him to take a walk!'

'Not precisely.'

'But you won't be dating him any more?'

'No.'

Emily grinned, and said again, thoughtfully, 'Aren't you the sly one? Don't worry, Brooke, I won't tell anyone. Your secret is safe with me.'

What secret? Brooke's head was already spinning with all that had happened this evening. She was in no mood to play along if Emily wanted to be mysterious.

I can't absorb another single thing tonight, she thought. But one thing was certain. Whatever secret Emily thought she knew, it certainly wasn't an unpleasant one. The girl was positively thrilled.

I'll wait, thought Brooke, and make her explain it to me in the morning. That will be time enough.

CHAPTER FIVE

By morning, though, Emily seemed to have forgotten all about it. 'What secret?' she queried, wide-eyed and innocent. 'Did I say something about a secret? I must have meant your secret plan to get rid of Dave.'

'You know darned well what you said, Emily.' Brooke was still in her robe; it was her day to work the evening shift at the library, so she normally slept a little later and went to work at noon. This morning, though, she had been up in plenty of time to see Tara off to school. Emily's mysterious secret had haunted her dreams; it was tormenting her now, and her mischievous younger sister was still pretending. Emily seemed to be convinced that she had stumbled across something that Brooke would love to keep hidden.

Was it Dave? she wondered. He and Emily had always got along so well that it was difficult to believe the girl would take their break-up so calmly.

Brooke had curled up on one of the sofas in the drawing-room with her coffee-cup. The sunshine spilling in through the long windows touched her hair and turned it almost butter-coloured.

Emily was sitting on the arm of a chair, perched as if she might suddenly fly away. No doubt she wanted to, Brooke thought drily. Whatever the young lady was up to, it boded no good for Brooke.

'Do you know, you look really pretty in that robe,' Emily added.

'Thanks. Now stop trying to change the subject. I don't know what makes you believe I'm concealing something, but I want to assure you I don't have any secrets.'

'Don't worry, Brooke. I won't tell a soul. In fact,' she added thoughtfully, 'I can't even remember what it is I promised not to tell.' She folded her hands angelically.

'Your halo is askew,' Brooke pointed out. She sighed and gave up. Obviously, Emily was not going to be shaken in her belief that she had solved a mystery. 'You don't seem upset that I won't be dating Dave any more.'

Emily shrugged. 'Not really. But I could pretend, if you'd like.'

'No, thanks. You seem to be doing enough pretending as it is. Will it make it difficult for you at work?'

'I don't think so. If it does, I'll just quit.'

Quit? With the summer barely started? Was this the same girl who had been working overtime to save up for college? Brooke was horrified. 'Emily, I don't know where you got the idea that you have a fortune to draw on, but you'll need every cent you can earn this summer. You can't quit——'

Emily swallowed a smile. 'I don't plan to quit,' she pointed out reasonably. 'I only said that I would if Dave gets impossible. He sometimes does, you know.'

'But you always seemed to like Dave.'

'I do like him, as a boss and as a tennis coach. It's as a brother-in-law that I wouldn't have been able to stomach him.'

'You never told me that.'

Emily waved a casual hand. 'Give me credit for a little conscience,' she said. 'It was you who would have to live with him, not me, and you seemed to think he was pretty special. Why should I make it tougher on you?'

'Why don't you like him?' Sharp-eyed Emily, Brooke thought. What else did she see that I didn't?

'Just little things. Besides . . . ' she looked a little shame-faced, 'I found out I have some of that Carlisle pride, too, and Dave just wasn't good enough for a classy lady like you. But what does it matter, now that you've given him the gate?' She glanced at her watch. 'I have to run, Brooke.'

'All right,' Brooke agreed reluctantly, wishing she could pick the girl up and shake the truth out to her.

'I left a letter on the breakfast table for you to look at,' Emily added. 'It's about orientation and tennis camp at Cedar. It's less than a month away, so we'll need to send the registration money soon.'

'I'll look it over,' Brooke promised. 'And I'll start a pot roast before I go to work, so dinner will be ready for you and Tara.'

'Thanks, love.' Emily jumped up, as if relieved to get out of the room. 'Though it's hardly fair to make you cook when you won't be home to enjoy it.'

'It's self-defence,' said Brooke. 'At least that way I know what Tara's eating.'

After Emily had gone, Brooke sat there for a long time, staring across the sunny drawing-room and out of the front windows. For the first time, she noticed that the curtains were showing faded streaks where the sun poured in on them day after day. She wondered if they would stand up to the autumn dry-cleaning, or if she'd have to replace them before the year was out. They'd cost a fortune to replace, that was certain; the windows were odd sizes and huge.

'I'll worry about that when the time comes,' she said firmly. If the worst came to the worst, they'd skip the cleaning. Better to have dusty curtains than none at all. It made her feel a little sad, though. Her mother would have taken one look at the streaks and telephoned the decorators for fabric samples. She had never spared expense where Oakley was involved, Brooke remembered, and she had always bought quality stuff.

But that had been in the old days, when there was still money for curtains and a housekeeper and a part-time gardener. Even last summer, near the end of Elliot's struggle to save the company when he had mortgaged everything he owned, they had called the teenager down the street whenever the lawn needed mowing, Brooke thought wearily as she climbed the maplewood staircase to get dressed. Now they did it themselves to save the cash outlay. That was her job for this morning, and heaven knew it would keep her occupied till it was time to go to work.

Her room was sunny and bright, the crisp yellow curtains adding to the brilliance of the light. She had worked so hard to create this island of peace, making the curtains herself, painting the walls. It had taken two weeks of hard work to get it just as she wanted it.

'Oh, stop it!' she told herself crossly. 'Stop feeling sorry for yourself because you don't have it easy. Taking care of Oakley is a full-time job, and it's one you chose!'

But she wondered about it, as she pushed the mower, trimming round bushes, trees and flower-beds. One of the oaks was showing no signs of life, she noted. Another bill for tree removal was all she needed!

Was Dave right? she asked herself. Had she taken on too big a job here, to try to keep Oakley Manor up by herself? Would she ultimately have to admit defeat? Would she finally be forced to sell her precious Oakley after all?

Never, she told herself. She gritted her teeth and pushed the mower a little faster.

Oakley, she thought. She could mortgage Oakley, and get the money for Emily's education. Ben Adams had told her he'd make her the loan, if only she had some collateral. Well, Oakley would be plenty of security, even if she had to borrow every dime of Emily's tuition.

But the very idea sent chills down her spine. From the day Grandfather Oakley had broken ground for the house, everything had been paid for before it was installed. He hadn't believed in borrowing money against his family's home, and he had passed on that determination. In three generations, there had never been a mortgage on Oakley. Brooke felt guilty just thinking about risking Oakley.

'But then again, there was never a need for a mortgage before now,' she told herself.

Her mother would have been horrified at the idea of borrowing money against the house. It was part of the reason, Brooke again recalled, that Oakley had been left to her and not to Elliot. If he had owned it, the house would have vanished along with the rest of his holdings, in his frantic, too-late struggle to save Carlisle Products.

'At least I still have it,' she told herself. 'And borrowing a few thousand dollars against it is hardly the same as letting it leave the family.'

Much as it hurt, it seemed the only thing she could do. She'd call Ben Adams as soon as she finished the front lawn, she decided. The sooner the better—then she could explain it to Emily.

Funny, she thought, that Emily hadn't been pestering her for details about the stock sale. She'd have expected that Emily would have demanded to see the cash by now. But then, she thought, Emily's mind is focused on Cedar College in the autumn. To the teenager, Carlisle Products was long gone and should be left to die.

Why did Ty have to come back to town? she asked herself miserably. That was what had really caused the trouble. Until he'd waved cash under Emily's nose, there had been no trouble. She would have gone to the junior college—not happily, but without protest, and done her best.

She still could, Brooke reminded herself. The confession would come hard and Emily would not easily forgive, but eventually she would understand.

And in the meantime? Brooke suppressed a little shiver at the idea of Bart Tipton. If Emily was capable of that, who knew what might come next? It was blackmail of a sort, of course, but it was also evidence of just how deeply Emily wanted to go to Cedar. If there was any way at all, Brooke knew, she could not deny her sister the chance to follow her dream.

Tyler Marshall had always been trouble, she thought, from the day when she had first realised how her insides seemed to melt whenever he looked at her. Even now, there was something about him that drew out the worst in her, some powerful force that made her struggle to defend herself from the attraction he still held for her.

All she had to do was think about that latest kiss, there in his hotel suite, and she was both furious and shaken. She could hardly make herself believe that he had the nerve to treat her like that. But even worse was the knowledge that she hadn't protested, that she had actually enjoyed those few moments in his arms. He certainly had a better technique these days, she told herself. He was gentle and self-assured, more than he had even been in the days of their engagement. Who, she wondered, had taught him that? Alison, perhaps? Or some other woman he had known in the last four years?

'You're sick, she thought. You're warped, even to be thinking about that kiss. How shaming it was that Ty's touch still had the power to make her uncomfortably aware of her body, of every sensitive nerve ending, when she knew perfectly well that it was a skill he had practised.

Well, at least thank heaven it wasn't likely to happen again. He'd made his point, there in the suite. There would be no repetition.

Brooke called the bank as soon as she had finished trimming the front lawn, but Ben Adams was out. She didn't leave her name; taking the loan would be bad enough, but letting word get out prematurely would be worse. She could catch him later.

She poured herself a glass of iced tea and sat down at the breakfast table to cool off. She was drenched with perspiration. The lawn was taking longer than she had expected; she would have to leave the back garden for the weekend. 'Just how I always wanted to to spend Sunday afternoon,' she muttered. 'Cutting grass.' But she couldn't do it this Sunday, she remembered abruptly. The library carnival was scheduled then, and she'd have to be there, wearing that darned T-shirt that was Jane's idea of a joke.

'In that case,' she told herself reluctantly, 'I'd better get back to work now, or it'll look like a jungle by next week.'

Tea in hand, she was almost at the front door when the bell rang. Who would be calling at this hour? she wondered, and decided that if it was a salesman, he'd get the surprise of his life. She had no time today to listen to terrific values in magazines, vacuum cleaners, chocolate, or any of the other wonders he might be peddling.

But when she opened the door, she found herself instantly wishing that it had been a salesman on her doorstep, instead of the man who was standing there, looking cool and trim in a grey linen suit, his silver hair touched by the sun.

'What do you want?' she asked curtly. 'I didn't invite you, and I don't want you here!'

'I did try the library first,' Ty Marshall said, 'if that makes you feel better.' He made a sweeping appraisal of her, from hot face to low-necked bloused, brief shorts and running shoes.

Brooke tried to ignore his gaze. She couldn't keep him from looking, that was for sure, she told herself. But she certainly didn't have to encourage him, by getting openly irritable about it. 'Well, try again this afternoon. You'll have better luck at finding me there.'

He braced a hand against the arched brick doorway and nodded. 'I quite understand your reluctance to talk to me this morning,' he said. 'I realise that you prefer having your private chats in public places.'

'What do you mean by that?'

'I was referring to the dressing down your friend Dave got last night at the club.' He paused, then added thoughtfully, 'I've always believed that social position and manners are supposed to go together. But if a lady feels no hesitation about treating a man like that in public . . . It almost makes me wonder if my aspirations make sense!'

Brooke hardly registered what he was saying. 'You heard all that?' she asked faintly.

'Most of it. My hearing is quite acute,' he added modestly. 'Tell me, did you smooth it over?'

'What makes you think it's any of your business?'

'Well, he did make a few references to Oakley Manor. It caught my attention. May I come in?'

'Why should I let you?'

'Because, regardless of your wishes, I still prefer to do business without an audience.'

'I don't have any business to transact with you.'

'But I do. Of course, I could make an exception if you insist, and discuss it at the library this afternoon.'

He would, too. Probably loudly, and in the centre of the main hall. Silently, Brooke pushed the door open.

The frozen look on her face didn't seem to bother him. 'Yes, I'd love a glass of tea,' he said. 'Thank you so much for offering.'

She would have poured hers over that well-pressed suit, except for one thing: she would be the one who would have to clean up the mess. She went to the kitchen.

He followed. 'You've changed the house very little,' he observed.

'Fortunately, Alison never succeeded in carrying out her plans for it,' Brooke said woodenly. 'If she had, I might as well have touched a match to it and started over.'

'That's a thought,' he conceded, and took a long drink of tea.

'You've lost me.'

'Torching the house,' he explained. 'You could collect the insurance that way, and solve your financial troubles.'

'I'm not in financial trouble.'

'Oh? I understand that you've been trying to raise money for Emily's education.'

And who, she wondered, had told him that? Ben Adams, of course. With their business dealings, they must be like old friends, trading inside information. She was abruptly glad that Ben hadn't been in the bank this morning, and that she hadn't yet made her request for the mortgage.

'May I sit down?' he asked, and did, before she could give permission. One of Tara's school drawings was lying on the breakfast table; he picked it up, looked at it expressionlessly, and laid it aside.

'I thought bankers had to be ethical,' Brooke said irritably. 'What ever happened to confidentiality?'

'There are ways and ways to get information,' he said. 'So you were trying to find some cash.'

Brooke shrugged. There was no point in denying it. 'Emily has chosen an expensive college,' she said shortly.

'And has the college chosen Emily?'

'Of course. In fact, they've offered her a partial scholarship, but tuition will still be high.'

'And you need cash,' he said gently.'

'You don't need to gloat over it,' snapped Brooke. 'If that's what you came for, you can leave any time.'

'But you told me a few days ago that you were doing

very well. So well, in fact, that you weren't interested in selling your stock.'

'Why do you care?' she challenged. 'Or are you just coming around now because you think you can buy it even cheaper?'

Ty shook his head sadly. 'You have so little faith in me, Brooke.'

'That's right. I know a snake when I see one. What are you offering now? Ten dollars a share?'

He thought about it. 'I don't think I'd be willing to go that high, actually,' he said finally. 'Unless, of course, we made a sort of package deal—all the stock, not just Emily's.'

'At that price? You must be joking!'

He shrugged. 'It was simply an offer.'

At that rate, she thought, all the shares would bring what he had once offered for Emily's alone. The total price would barely pay for Emily's first year at Cedar. What would they do next year, then? There would be nothing to fall back on. No, there was no point in even considering it.

'Your so-called offer is an insult,' she said tartly. 'If I wanted to give the stock away, I'd have a raffle or something. I wouldn't just meekly hand it over to you, and then tell you thanks for taking it off my hands!'

'Oh, I quite understand the position it puts you in,' he said. 'But at the moment that's all it's worth to me.' He sipped his tea and looked her over. 'I see only a few options for you, Brooke.'

He sounded concerned, she thought. What an actor he was! 'Thanks awfully, but I'd prefer to think of my own solutions.'

He didn't seem to hear her. 'That's good tea,' he said. 'Do you mind if I help myself to more?'

'Please don't. If you've said what you came here for——'

'I haven't.' But he didn't continue.

Brooke sighed and stood up. 'Very well. I'll get you more tea. But at the end of this glass, you're leaving!' She packed it with ice, leaving as little room as possible for liquid.

'Really?' he asked mildly. 'And are you going to throw me out?'

'It is my house,' she pointed out.

'That's what I wanted to talk to you about,' he said, as if delighted that she finally understood.

She set the glass down in front of him with a bang.

'The way it looks to me, Brooke,' he confided, 'you have a problem. Cedar College—I will say this about Emily; she has good taste. Cedar has the best pre-law programme anywhere in the state.'

'I'm so glad it has your approval,' Brooke said tightly.

'But on your salary . . . ' He shook his head. 'Emily is an expensive luxury, and you have no resources left to draw on.'

'Must you sound so happy about it?' The words were goaded from her.

'I could shed a few crocodile tears if it would make you feel better. Or did you expect me to feel real sympathy?' His eyes were suddenly cold.

No, she thought. After the way I've been treating you as if you were less than human—no, I didn't expect real sympathy. But neither do I have to listen to this!

'It seems to me that you have a couple of choices, Brooke. I'm sure you're considered selling Oakley, to raise the money.'

'Never!' The word flashed from her, sharp and vehement.

Ty smiled. 'The speed of that answer tells me that you have, indeed, thought about it. But perhaps you've hesitated because there aren't many people in this town who want a house the size of Oakley, or who could afford to pay what it's worth.'

'I don't want to sell it!'

'That, my dear, is an entirely different question. How much money will you take?' Their eyes met across the table.

'The house is not for sale,' repeated Brooke.

'Name your price.' His tone was soft, but there was no denying the hardness that lay under it.

'Ten million dollars!' she snapped, goaded into impatience.

Ty's gaze didn't waver. 'A little steep, don't you think? Never mind—we've now established that Oakley Manor has a price, so we can begin negotiating on it.'

'I will never sell you this house, Ty Marshall. I'd hang myself from the beams in the front hall first!'

'A bit short-sighted, I'd say.' He didn't sound particularly interested. 'I'd simply buy it from Emily and Tara, probably for much less than I'd give you.'

She stared at him for a long moment. 'Why do you want Oakley?' she asked at last.

'That, my dear Brooke, is none of your business.'

'Revenge, I suppose. You want to hand the Carlisles a knock-out blow.'

He smiled. 'Regardless of what you think, I have nothing against Carlisles, singly or en masse.'

'You seem to have plenty against me,' she murmured.

His eyes flared with humour. 'Yes, but that's not because you're a Carlisle. That's simply a matter of personality.' He looked around admiringly. 'I've always liked this house.'

'You will never own it.' Brooke stood up. 'I have to go to work. If you would leave now . . . ?'

Ty stayed motionless. 'Of course, you could put a mortgage on it,' he confided. 'It would raise the necessary funds, and you could pay the loan back over the next twenty or thirty years.'

'That's right,' she agreed crisply. 'I could.' He didn't sound terribly upset at the idea, she thought, and wondered why. If she did that, it would mean that Oakley would escape his grasp—wouldn't it?

'Of course, banks don't hold mortgage loans for all those long years,' he murmured. 'They resell the paper as soon as they can, to other companies or private investors. It would be no great challenge for me to end up holding the mortgage on Oakley Manor.'

'So what? I'd pay it back.'

'Oh, I'm sure you'd be an excellent risk. But what happens if you get sick, Brooke, and can't work? What happens if your expenses are higher than usual, and you have to miss a payment? Oakley needs work right now, and if it's put off, it will cost even more. What happens if you lose your job?' He looked at her thoughtfully, and added, 'I've always wanted to be on the board of directors of a library.'

And if he was, Brooke thought bitterly, he just might manage to get her fired.

'No,' he went on, 'all I'd have to do would be to buy up the paper and wait for you to stumble, and then I'd have it after all.'

She looked down at her fingers, clenched together in her lap to stop them trembling. He was ruthless enough to do it, she knew. But why would he warn her of what he intended? Why hadn't he just let her walk unseeing into that trap? Unless—unless he was arranging an even bigger trap.

'What do you really want, Tyler?' she asked.

Reluctant respect flared in his eyes. 'You're quick, aren't you, Brooke?'

'No. I just know you better than you think.' Her voice was hard. Her illusions were quickly vanishing.

'Let's call it a package deal, shall we? I really don't want to own that stock, but I'll loan Emily—and Tara when her turn comes—all the money they need for college, against the value of the stock.'

'Which, at the moment, is nothing,' snapped Brooke.

'True. But it doesn't have to stay that way. Carlisle Products will make money again—if I choose to reopen it.'

'And when are you going to make that choice?'

'That depends on you, Brooke,' he said gently. 'The package includes the business. If the arrangement I'm offering doesn't suit you, the building will sit there shuttered and padlocked until the roof falls in, and your stock will be worth precisely nothing.'

'But you must have planned to do something with it. You've invested thousands of dollars.'

'That's right. But you see, I can survive without that money. Can you?'

Of course I can, she thought. But I have to admit it would be a lot easier with it.

'And if I agree?' she said. 'Emily gets her education in exchange for her share of the company?'

'It would be a fair enough trade, don't you think? Actually, I wouldn't insist on owning the stock. As a matter of fact, I'd even be willing to consider it a loan that will never be repaid.'

It sounded like a generous offer. Far too generous, Brooke thought. The price was going to be steep.

'What's in it for you?' she asked suspiciously. 'Not the stock—you could have that right now for far less than Emily's education will cost, let alone Tara's. And you're not a philanthropist, looking for a good cause. So—what is it?'

Ty drained his tea glass and set it aside. 'Oakley,' he said.

'No!' It came straight from the heart. 'I will not sell you Oakley!'

He lifted a dark eyebrow. 'As I recall,' he said, 'a few minutes ago, I offered to buy it, and you refused. I haven't renewed my offer.'

Horror dawned in her. 'You want me to give Oakley to you, in exchange?'

'Oh, no. Not that you'd really be giving it to me,' he added. 'I'd be taking it. But we can discuss it at another time. You need to go to work, and I did agree to leave after that glass of tea. Thank you. Perhaps after you leave work tonight?'

He was almost at the front door when she caught up with him. 'I think we'll finish it now,' she said. 'What are you suggesting? You're certainly not picking up the tab for college and law school out of the goodness of your heart.'

'Oh, no,' he said pleasantly. 'Do you use this little study much, by the way?' He stepped through the doorway of the small booklined room, its walnut panelling softly glowing.

Brooke followed him in reluctantly, remembering the

day she had thrown her diamond ring at him here. 'Seldom.'

'Why? Too many unpleasant memories?'

'What do memories have to do with anything? What's the price, Tyler?'

There was a pause, then he turned to look down at her. 'Remember what you said last night about family?' he said softly. 'And good breeding? And how acceptance can only be earned over a long period of time?'

'Yes,' she whispered. It had been awful of her to say those things. But surely he wouldn't exact this dreadful price of her, simply because she had once again reminded him that he had grown up on the wrong side of the tracks. Surely——

There was nothing sure about it, she reminded herself. Ty Marshall was as capable as any of holding a grudge. And he certainly had reason to want to see Brooke Carlisle smashed in the dust.

'But there's another way to earn social standing, Brooke,' he said. 'A way I'm surprised you didn't think of last night. I may not be able to earn those things overnight for myself, but I can ensure them for—the future.'

'How?' Her voice was a bare thread.

There was a faint light of sympathy in his eyes, but none in his words. 'By marrying someone who already has them, Brooke.'

She tried to swallow, but there was suddenly a rock in her throat. 'Marrying—do you mean me?' she croaked.

'Who else? Tara is a a little young, and Emily has other plans.'

The words dropped into a silence in the room. Brooke couldn't speak. She shook her head numbly.

Ty raised a dark eyebrow. 'You sound shocked,' he observed. 'After all, you did agree to marry me, once. It's hardly a new idea.'

'That's why you proposed to me before, too, isn't it?' she said. 'For Oakley, and the Carlisles' position . . . '

'Something like that.' He didn't sound interested.

'Well, I won't marry you,' she said. 'I absolutely refuse.'

Unbidden came the thought of Emily. Who had told him Emily was going to law school? Brooke had never mentioned that to Ben Adams, she was certain. She had never told him which college Emily wanted to attend. And yet Ty knew, without question he knew—Emily!

'Don't act hastily, my dear,' he advised. 'And I'd suggest that you have a good story prepared for Emily, if you decide to turn me down. She'll be very disappointed, I'd afraid, if her college education is sacrificed.'

'She did talk to you!' Brooke breathed.

'Of course she did. She was terribly upset with me at first, because I hadn't bought the stock, until I explained the new plan. It just didn't seem ethical, you see, if I was to profit because she had to sell out prematurely. But since I'll be part of the family, it would be only appropriate for me to help her through school.'

'You told her that?' Brooke was almost screaming.

Ty lifted an eyebrow. 'Of course I told her,' he said gently. 'Why on earth should I keep such happy news a secret? Can Emily keep a secret, by the way?'

'Oh, yes,' she said bitterly.

He seemed not to hear; his attention had gone on to other things. 'I like this study,' he said. 'I think I'll use it for my office, since you're not terribly fond of it.'

'I won't marry you!'

He didn't seem to hear. He was studying the view from the bay window.

'Tyler, why?' she called after him. 'Surely you don't expect me to believe you're still in love with me!'

'Love? Do you really think that's what we felt for each other? I had no idea you were so idealistic.' He shook his head. 'No, I don't expect you to believe that.'

'Then why this proposal?'

For a moment she thought he wasn't going to answer her at all. Then he came across the study to her. 'Fitting, isn't it?' he said. 'That we're talking about it in this room, I mean. Something like returning to the scene of the crime.'

'Ty——'

'To answer your question, I want to marry you because

you still have many of the things I've always wanted, and marriage is the only way to get them. I'm willing to pay the price.' He let his fingers slide gently along the line of her throat.'

She pulled away from his touch. 'And put up with a wife who despises you?' she whispered. 'Are you willing to pay that price, too?'

Ty shook his head. 'I don't think you despise me, Brooke,' he said. 'You're not a cold woman, yet you've never married. I think it's because you haven't found a man who knows how to set you on fire.'

'And you think you can?'

'I know I can.' His hands cupped her face and turned it up to him. 'And you have not forgotten—any more than I have.'

She shivered under the dark glow of his eyes. 'And that's enough for you?'

He shrugged and let her go. 'It keeps a man warm on a winter night. What more can he ask? I shan't let you be cold, Brooke.'

'I told you, no. Absolutely, without question, no.'

He was at the front door by then, and he didn't answer.

She followed him into the hallway. 'Did you hear me?' she cried.

Ty turned, one hand braced on the door, unsmiling. 'I heard you, Brooke. Let me know when you change your mind.'

CHAPTER SIX

BROOKE stood there in the hall for a moment after Ty had gone, swaying under the shock. Then she tottered into the little study and sat down on the edge of a chair, huddled into a heap with her arms folded tightly.

It didn't happen, she told herself. Ty wasn't here. He didn't say those things. He didn't demand that I make a sacrifice of myself on the altar of his ambition and Emily's future . . .

Receiving a proposal of marriage is supposed to make a woman happy, she told herself. Not deliriously joyful, of course, as it might have in the Victorian days when an innocent maiden never allowed herself to dream of her suitor as a husband. Sometimes such a maiden even fainted with shock when the question was actually asked. But in these modern days, a proposal was never unexpected.

Well, this one had been a surprise, Brooke told herself grimly. And far from a pleasant one, at that. If, indeed, it was accurate to refer to it as a proposal. Calling it a blackmail demand would be closer to the mark.

She put her head back against the chair cushion. A single hot tear seeped from the corner of her eye. 'Dad always told me that quick tongue of mine would get me in trouble,' she whispered, and forced herself to face up to what she had said last night at the club. Was that when Tyler had made his decision? Had that been why he had been in such good humour, and sent the Martini to her table—because he had decided to take his revenge this way?

'Why did I have to say those things?' she asked herself, her voice rising in near-hysteria. 'I brought this mess on myself. Why couldn't I have just been quiet? After that attack, anyone but a saint would have demanded revenge!'

But perhaps a desire for revenge was all it was! She grasped at the possibility. Maybe Tyler hadn't meant any of that stuff he had talked about, and all he wanted was to watch her squirm, to enjoy toying with her as she struggled to find a way out. There must be some sort of sadistic pleasure for him in thinking that he had her in his power, that the proud and respected Brooke Carlisle was grovelling and begging to be released from this trap.

She had stabbed at his pride when she had rejected him and broken their engagement. She had done so again in the last few days. Perhaps this was only his way of getting even.

If that was so, then she could turn the tables. If she stopped fighting him, and meekly agreed to his terms, Ty would be stunned, and suddenly he would be the one scrambling for a way out! The thought made her smile.

But the humour soon died, as she realised he must have been planning this for days. She had come straight back to Oakley from the club last night, and Emily had obviously known about the supposed engagement before Brooke had come in. Tyler had still been at the club then, so Emily must have talked to him earlier in the day. The exchange at the club last night couldn't have been the force that had ignited this morning's madness, after all.

It was some relief, she thought, that she hadn't brought this horror down upon herself with her quick tongue.

Brooke forced herself to consider the terms Ty had offered. If she accepted his proposal, Emily would benefit. So would Tara, less directly. He obviously didn't intend this to be a temporary measure, either, she mused, if he was already planning to finance Tara's education as well. That was still nearly ten years in the future.

But it should come as no surprise, she told herself. He had wanted to marry her, once, long before hurt and anger and revenge had come into it. And he had said himself that she represented things he wanted, and that marriage was simply the price he must pay to have them . . .

And what of Brooke herself? Could she bear to spend

ten years as Ty Marshall's wife? A decade of sharing a house with him, making a home with him? Once, she had planned to spend her life with him, looked forward to being his wife. But now?

Was he right? she asked herself. The way she felt when he had kissed her that night in his hotel suite—was that only the embers of the passion she had once felt for him? If she married him, would she be able to bear the travesty of the love she had once been so certain they shared? Could she live with him, sleep with him as he so obviously intended, and feel as she did?

'At Oakley,' she reminded herself. 'At least I'd get to keep Oakley.'

But how foolish, she thought, to assume that he could so easily take Oakley from her! It was hers, and as long as she didn't mortgage it, there would be no way he could gain control of the house. He couldn't walk in and take her home away just because he wanted it.

A weight seemed to have lifted from her shoulders, and she ran up the stairs, cheerful again. The whole morning's conversation had been just another example of Ty's skill at manipulating people. He had taken a few facts and added a good dose of spellbinding charm, and for a few minutes she had actually believed that there might be no other solution than to do as he demanded. How foolish of her to think that he might have that sort of power!

To marry him—to submit herself to him——Cold shivers ran up her spine, despite the warmth of the room. He hadn't even laid a finger on her this morning, but his gaze had made her feel branded. To be his wife under terms like those—it was a good thing for her that there was another answer.

She closed her eyes under the shower spray, and suddenly the water sliding over her skin felt like a warm hand stroking her, like Tyler had that day in his hotel room, when he had kissed her.

The memory of the kiss brought hot colour to her face. The worst part of it, she thought, was that she had actually enjoyed him touching her, kissing her. She groaned, wishing she had not allowed her curiosity to push her into his arms that day. To marry him—to give him the right to hold her like that!

'I won't,' she said aloud. 'I simply can't. And it isn't necessary, anyway.'

It wasn't until she was out of the shower and almost dressed that she realised how absurdly simple she had made it all sound. But it would not be that easy. Brooke wouldn't dare chance putting a mortgage on Oakley now. He had told her that if she did, he would find a way to take the house from her, and she believed he would do it through fair means or foul.

But she had no other way of raising money. If she refused Ty's proposal, Emily would have settle for junior college, after all. She would have to live at home to cut expenses, and she would have to keep working frantically to save so she could go on to the state university in two years' time.

And Emily was not the only one who would suffer. If Brooke refused this proposal, it would mean that Carlisle Products would remain closed, empty, non-productive. Not only would there never be a return from the stock the three sisters owned, it would mean that workers would remain jobless and the payroll that had meant so much to this little town would never to restored.

'Look,' she told herself fiercely, 'you can't be responsible for the whole damned town! No one will ever know you had anything to do with it!'

Unless Tyler told someone, which he was quite capable of doing. 'I was going to reopen that plant,' he would say, 'if Brooke had married me. But since she turned me down, I'll have to mend my broken heart somewhere else. I couldn't bear to run the factory now . . . ' Oh, he'd have an explanation, that was for sure—and he would not hesitate to smear her reputation as thoroughly as only Ty was capable of doing.

She didn't doubt, either, that he was financially able to let Carlisle Products sit there and rot. He would never miss the thousands of dollars that he had invested, and he could be ruthless enough to leave the town behind without a thought of the damage he had done.

With all the evidence before her, did she even have a choice? 'If I do,' she told herself bitterly, 'it's because Ty slipped up somewhere along the line.'

The important thing right now, she thought, was to find out where he might have made some mistake, some tiny miscalculation, that would let her find a way out. For she knew, with a sinking sensation deep inside her, that if she didn't discover a loophole she would probably be Mrs Tyler Marshall before another month went by.

Sunday morning dawned sunny and warm. Brooke woke to find Tara sitting on the foot of her bed, patiently staring at her. She groaned and pulled a pillow over her head. 'Tara, for heaven's sake go away. It's barely light outside!'

'It's carnival day,' Tara explained patiently.

'I know. But that's not till afternoon.'

'I promised Jane I'd help her with the games for the little kids.' Tara sounded deadly serious. 'I have to be there early.'

Brooke took the pillow off her face and sat up. Since when, she wondered idly, had Tara decided she was no longer a little kid herself?

'Not this early,' she said.

But Tara just looked at her silently, her big blue eyes pleading.

Brooke gave in. 'All right. But we're at least having breakfast first,' she ordered. 'I cannot face a carnival without eating.'

'They're having chilli dogs,' Tara volunteered.

'Good. You may have as many as you can stand for lunch. Now, run along while I get dressed.' It was punctuated with a yawn; Brooke hadn't slept well. That was another thing Ty Marshall could take credit for, she thought glumly. She had scarcely slept in three days, since he had come to Oakley that morning with his ultimatum.

Tara shook her head. 'You'll just go back to sleep as soon as I'm gone. I'm not leaving till you're up.'

Reluctantly, Brooke pushed the sheet back. 'All right, I'm up. Why don't you go work on waking Emily?'

'She's impossible,' Tara announced, and vanished down the hall.

Brooke hunted out a pair of white shorts and the T-shirt that Jane had insisted on giving her. 'Fiction readers are novel lovers,' she muttered. 'Jane has a sick sense of humour. The whole thing is a waste of time, anyway—the very idea of a carnival is a useless one.'

By the middle of the afternoon, however, she had changed her mind. Useless was no longer the word she would have chosen; frantic might have been closer. It seemed to her that the entire town had turned out to play bingo, eat ice cream, and rummage through the table of bargain books that Jane had been collecting. Across the park, people were lined up to throw a ball at a tiny target in the hope of dumping the Mayor into a vat of cold water. Jane was manning the Friend's booth with a megaphone and a continual stream of chatter about the advantages of being a volunteer. Brooke herself was selling tickets which could be exchanged for food, games and chances at the Mayor, and it seemed to her that she hadn't had time for a deep breath all afternoon.

Dave was there. He'd stopped to speak to her, and Brooke had thought he looked very sad. Astonishing, she thought, that in the last few days she'd given no thought at all to Dave. She hadn't even missed him. But then her whole mind had been focused on finding a way to outwit Ty Marshall.

Ty, she thought, was the only person in Oakley Mills who wasn't in the park today. She wondered if he was watching the fun from his hotel room. She felt like looking up towards Suite 500 and sticking her tongue out at the windows overlooking the park, just on the chance that he was standing there and watching her.

Tara appeared at the ticket table. Her shorts and shirt were crumpled and stained with ice cream, and her freckled nose was beginning to sunburn, Brooke saw. Ah well, she thought. We'll all look like peeling lobsters in the morning.

It brought back a shade of longing for the years when she was a teenager. Then she'd had endless hours to lie in the early summer sun and gradually build up a deep, even tan that highlighted her blonde hair and green eyes. Now she was too busy, and lawn-mowing and gardening had to do double duty.

'I ran out of tickets,' Tara announced.

'What do you mean, you ran out? I just bought you five dollars' worth.' Brooke counted out a customer's change, smiled, and welcomed him to the festival.

'I used them all on chilli dogs,' Tara admitted.

'All of them?' asked Brooke with foreboding. 'You ate five chilli dogs?'

'You said I could have as many as I liked. And I was hungry.'

'I should have known better,' muttered Brooke. 'In that case, where did you get the ice cream?'

'Mr Marshall bought it for me.' Tara waved her hand toward the food tent.

Brooke's hand jerked, and she had to stoop to retrieve a handful of change from the grass. When she stood up again, her face was pink. Sure enough, there was Ty, a hundred feet or so from her. She felt a little breathless.

It was the first time since he'd come back to town that she had seen him so casually dressed. Even when she'd seen him at the club, he'd been wearing well-tailored golfing clothes. But today it was jeans and running shoes, far more like the Tyler she remembered. She hadn't noticed before, she thought, quite how much he had changed.

'He's nice,' Tara volunteered.

'When it suits his purpose,' muttered Brooke. She scrawled her name on an IOU, dropped it into the cashbox, and handed Tara another batch of tickets. 'You may start by paying Mr Marshall back,' she suggested.

'He bought me some lemonade too,' added Tara.

'Great.' But what had he paid the bill with? Brooke wondered. She had been at the ticket table all day, and she hadn't seem him. Or had he been there during the rush, when she had scarcely seen the people she had been selling tickets to? Had she touched him, perhaps even put her hand almost in his and been unaware of it?

Normally, she thought, that kind of prudish thinking would never even have occurred to her. But with Ty, one never knew. He was capable of putting any sort of interpretation on the simplest things.

She watched as Tara skipped back across the park, and saw the child tuck her hand confidingly into Tyler's. With the other hand, she gestured towards one of the games, and obligingly, he started off in that direction.

'Well,' said Jane from the next table. She had put her megaphone down for the moment, and her voice sounded slightly hoarse. 'He acts as if she's his responsibility.' Her eyes held a flicker of curiosity.

'I hadn't noticed,' Brooke said tightly.

'Perhaps you'd better pay a little more attention.' Then Jane relented. 'You've had a steady line here, haven't you?'

'It's finally died down, thank heaven. I can't believe it's possible that we've raised so much money.'

'I know. But it was a heck of a lot of work,' said Jane. 'Next year, what if we just do something simple?'

Brooke looked at her with foreboding. 'That depends on your definition of simple,' she said. 'As I recall, you promised me this carnival would be a breeze.'

'It's been worth it,' Jane assured her. 'For our next project, I was thinking in terms of a cookbook. I have a sure-fire idea for one.'

Brooke sold another booklet of tickets, then perched on the edge of the table. 'I can't wait,' she said. 'Tell me about it.'

'How to Feed a Family of Four by Investing Twenty Minutes a Day and Twenty Dollars a Week,' Jane declaimed.

'The title is too long.'

Jane shrugged it off. 'So we'll call it the Twenty-Twenty Cookbook.'

'Then people will think it's a list of recipes to improve your eyesight, using carrots. Why not just call it the

Miracle Cookbook? With those rules, it would be a
miracle if a recipe qualified.'

'It was only a thought,' said Jane. 'I never claimed that
the bugs were all worked out.' She picked up her megaphone again, and then lowered it. 'Hey, isn't that Bart
Tipton over there with Emily?'

'Oh, no.' Brooke looked around, and spotted them at
the cake-stall. Bart had apparently won a layer cake, and
he was consuming it by the handful, without bothering to
cut it into slices. As Brooke watched, he scooped up a
fingerful of frosting and smeared it on Emily's chin, then
leaned towards her as if to kiss it off. To Emily's credit,
she stepped away, but Bart seemed determined. He drew
the cake back as if to smear the whole thing in her face,
and Emily shrieked and started to run.

That has to stop, thought Brooke, furious. She would
have expected something of the sort from Bart Tipton,
but Emily ought to know better than to behave like a
hoodlum in public. But what on earth could Brooke do
about it? She couldn't even leave the ticket table, and
Emily wasn't fool enough to come anywhere close. She
knew what Brooke would have to say about such behaviour.

Emily hadn't had much to say for the last several days,
and Brooke had been avoiding her sister as much as
possible. She was determined not to talk to Emily about
the supposed engagement until she knew exactly what she
was going to say; it didn't take a genius to figure out that
anything Emily knew would go straight back to Tyler.
And Brooke was not ready to make her stand yet. She
hadn't found the key to release her from this prison, but
she wasn't giving up searching. And so she hadn't challenged Emily's pert assumption that the engagement was
real and Brooke was, for some mysterious reason, trying
to keep it a secret.

But she was beginning to feel a little desperate. So far,
Ty hadn't bothered her. She hadn't even seen him in the
last three days, but she could never quite rid herself of
the idea that he was watching, from somewhere just out

of her sight, waiting for her to trip, so he could swoop in like a hyena for the kill.

Which pretty well expressed her ideas of what marriage to him would be like, she thought glumly. She just had to come up with some good ideas very, very soon.

She looked up to see Emily in front of the table. 'I'm sorry,' the girl said. The amazing thing was, Brooke thought, that Emily actually looked sorry. She stood, head bent, eyes downcast.

'Where's Bart?' asked Brooke. 'Not that I expect any indication of remorse from him——'

'He left.' Irrepressible Emily stifled a tiny giggle. 'You should have seen him, Brooke. Ty told him he didn't look very tough with frosting all over his hands and face, and Bart just kind of melted into a puddle and slunk away.'

Tyler again. 'I wish he'd keep out of my business,' Brooke muttered, and instantly regretted it.

Emily looked startled. 'Whatever do you mean?' she asked. 'It was great.'

'Oh?' Brooke's tone was dry. 'I can hear what you'd have said if I had interfered.'

Emily shrugged. 'Ty's different. Bart would have laughed at you, but he took one look at Tyler and decided he didn't want to find out whether he's as strong as he looks.'

'I would never have suspected Bart of having so much sense,' said Brooke drily.

At the Friends' booth, Jane was back in full voice. 'We're an organisation of women, we Friends of the Library. Men, it's an ideal place to meet the ladies, for your annual dues of only five dollars. How about some of you men joining? We can use your strong backs!'

'Not a bad idea,' a man called from across the park. 'But is that all you're offering for my five bucks? A chance to show off my muscles?'

Jane's grin flashed. 'Of course not,' she fired back. 'For all you men, I'm offering a special deal. An incentive for joining. Any man paying his dues in the next ten minutes will receive a kiss from our very own luscious blonde Brooke!'

Brooke swung round to the neighbouring table. Emily was forgotten. 'Jane, what are you trying to do to me?' she wailed.

'Be a sport, Brooke. It's all in a good cause,' Jane hissed.

The man who had asked the question strolled up to the table. 'If that's what the deal is' he drawled, 'here's a ten-spot. I'll take two.'

Brooke clenched her fist at Jane. But, she thought, what harm could it do? A little sport for the library—and heaven knew the Friends' treasury could use the money. 'Give the gentleman his change, Jane,' she ordered.

'Kissing booth rules,' added Jane, pocketing the cash. 'Mind your manners, guys. Make an orderly line, now.'

'Boy,' Emily muttered under her breath. 'And you were ready to scream at me for what I did?' She stalked away as if offended.

Jane's special deal, Brooke saw with a sinking heart, had achieved plenty of attention. Some of the men already in line were heckling friends standing around. Each dropped his money into Jane's hand, gave Brooke an enthusiastic kiss, and got his volunteer pin.

'Look at this!' chortled Jane, holding up the bills. 'Brooke, you've done more for the Friends in ten minutes than the membership committee has all year!'

'Don't get any ideas,' Brooke ordered.

The line had died down when a twenty-dollar bill floated to the table in front of Jane. 'Ah,' she said wisely, looking at her customer. 'I wondered when you'd be along. Here's your change.'

'Consider it dues paid in advance,' said Ty Marshall. 'I hate to fuss about these things every year.'

So he had no intention of leaving town, had he? Brooke thought. Or was this, too, just for show, to illustrate to her how certain he was that she would agree to his demands?

Jane smiled. 'I thought perhaps you wanted four times as much of Brooke's attention,' she said demurely.

Brooke tried to brace herself so she could appear

unmoved, but she was suddenly shivering instead. 'I can't,' she said under her breath.

'Why not?' he asked sombrely. 'You've kissed a dozen others.'

'That was different.' It wasn't until she saw the sparkle in his grey eyes that she saw her words had more than one interpretation. 'I don't want to kiss you, dammit——' she hissed.

'But if you don't, you'll call a lot of attention to yourself.'

'And you'd make certain everyone knew it too, wouldn't you?' Brooke said bitterly. She stood on tiptoe and brushed her lips against his cheek. The contact seemed to burn her mouth. 'There. You've had your kiss.'

Ty smiled gently at her. 'That was hardly worthy of the name,' he said. 'Don't worry, I'll be happy to collect a little later. Personally, I prefer privacy when I kiss a lovely woman.'

Did he really think she was lovely? she wondered idly. Though it couldn't possibly matter. He hadn't proposed to her because of her looks, that was for sure. No matter what she looked like, she had the social standing he wanted. That was the only thing that really mattered to Ty Marshall. The sexual attraction he felt for her was a side benefit.

'When may I expect an answer?' he added quietly. 'I've been waiting for three days now——'

'And you can wait three years for all I care!' snapped Brooke.

'But Emily doesn't have three years,' he reminded her. 'Or even three months.'

Brooke's hands clenched till her nails cut ridges in her palms. His assessment was too accurate, she thought. What chance did she have of escaping him?

'If you're looking for a way out,' he added, 'let me assure you that the only choice you have is to confess everything to Emily and then take a vow of poverty. It's something I can't quite imagine you doing, Brooke.'

'Let me tell you this, Mr Marshall,' she flared, 'I will

never marry you because of money! Money isn't all-important——'

'Until you run out of it,' he reflected. 'Then sometimes it's very important indeed.'

'You certainly seem to put a great deal of emphasis on it,' she said bitterly, and deliberately added, 'It's an attitude that is typical of your sort of person.'

'It's not the money itself,' he said. 'Money is just paper, after all, or numbers on a page—something that people are willing to trade valuable things for. All money means to me is what it will buy.'

His eyes summed her up, leaving little doubt in her mind as to what he meant.

'Well, I'm not for sale,' she said gruffly.

'I wasn't proposing to purchase you, exactly,' Ty said mildly. 'I'm merely trying to solve your problems and mine at the same time.'

Emily reappeared. 'There you are, Ty,' she said. 'I haven't had a chance to ask her. Brooke, Ty said he'd give me the money for my orientation workshop and tennis camp. It has to be sent in tomorrow, and I won't get paid till the end of the week. But he said I had to check with you, to see if it was all right.' Obviously she saw nothing wrong with the idea and was slightly puzzled at having to ask.

How much I would give, Brooke thought, to be able to reach into my pocket and hand her the hundred dollars! But she didn't have it any more than Emily did, and furthermore, she couldn't spare it this week. If it didn't come from Tyler, then there would be no orientation session for Emily at all.

Brooke looked up, and her green eyes met Ty's grey ones across the ticket table. Damn you, Tyler Marshall, she wanted to say, and she knew he could read the thought.

'I can go, can't I?' asked Emily. Her voice was slightly breathless, as if she were on the verge of panic.

Brooke's choices flashed before her eyes, as clearly as if they'd been written in neon. Emily with Bart Tipton, or Emily with a Cedar College education and a law degree. Tara with a series of makeshift babysitters, or in the special summer camps Brooke herself had gone to. Oakley with its deteriorating curtains and shaggy grounds, or Oakley well kept, sparkling again as it had been in her mother's day.

And me? Brooke thought. What about me? Working and fretting about making the payments, or financially comfortable—with Ty.

Being comfortable with Ty—it was a contradiction in terms. And yet, she thought, there were things he wanted from this marriage too. It wouldn't all be one-sided, because she had some bargaining power as well.

'Brooke?' asked Emily. The thin edge of panic in her voice was growing.

But Brooke didn't look at Emily. She met Tyler's eyes, her chin lifted proudly, and said quietly, 'Yes, Emily. Of course you'll go.'

And she knew as she said it that her life could never be the same again.

CHAPTER SEVEN

EMILY'S sigh was heartfelt. 'Well, that's a relief,' she said. 'I was beginning to wonder. Hey,' she added, suspicion clouding her face, 'you aren't trying to keep something away from me, are you? You two are still engaged, aren't you? You haven't broken up again?'

Jane's head turned. 'Did I hear somebody say "engaged"?' she asked.

Brooke looked up into Ty's unsmiling face. Obviously he wasn't going to confirm or deny, she thought. It was just another piece of the humiliation for her to be the one who had to announce that they would soon be married.

She wanted to run away and hide, or to scream that she was being blackmailed into this farce of a marriage. But she knew that if she were to hold up her head in the future, she must maintain her dignity now. To tell Emily the truth would accomplish nothing; it would merely make them both unhappy. It was very important for Emily to believe that this engagement had been Brooke's idea as much as Ty's. She had to be convinced that Brooke would be happy in her marriage.

Brooke sucked in a deep breath. 'Yes, you did, Jane,' she said, with a calm voice that astonished her. 'And of course we're still engaged, Emily. Whatever made you think differently?'

It was the first time she had ever seen Jane speechless. The woman opened and closed her mouth several times before finally saying, 'In that case, Ty, I think we should refund the charge for that kiss!'

Ty waved it away. 'Believe me,' he said, not taking his eyes off Brooke, 'my fiancée will make it worthwhile —after the carnival, of course.'

Brooke closed her eyes for an instant, in silent relief.

She hadn't even realised it until he had spoken, but she had been afraid that he would raise an enquiring eyebrow and deny all knowledge of an engagement. It would have been perfect vengeance, she thought, to humiliate her in front of a crowd. But then Ty was playing for no small stakes. Petty embarrassment wouldn't satisfy him.

And why should I feel relieved? she asked herself. That's stupid. I wish he'd denied it! I'd have suffered through a few weeks of public discomfort because I'd been jilted, and then it would all have been over. Now it will go on for years.

Black fear washed over her. Now that she was committed, now that it was too late to back out, she was horrified by what she had done. Tyler saw the expression in her eyes. Suddenly his hand was firm under her elbow, providing support and reminding her at the same time that there was no escape from him now.

Emily gave her a quick kiss. 'I'm so glad,' she said. 'I'm going home now so I can get those forms ready to mail.'

'Why don't you take Tara with you?' Ty suggested.

'Do I have to?' Then Emily relented. 'All right, I guess, since the lovebirds want to be alone.'

'That's right,' Ty agreed. 'I might even talk Brooke into letting you have her car.'

Brooke didn't bother to argue. She flipped the keys at Emily. 'I'll be home as soon as the mess is cleaned up,' she said.

Jane was shaking her head. 'I have it all handled,' she said. 'My clean up crews will take care of everything. Go ahead, honey. You've been working all day.'

'So have you.'

'But I'm not celebrating my engagement. Lucky girl!' added Jane, with an arch glance at Tyler. 'Take her home, Ty, before she falls over with fatigue.'

'I'd noticed she was getting a little pale,' Ty agreed calmly.

As if he didn't know what had caused her pallor! Brooke wanted to kick him in the shin, just to see if he had any sort of feelings at all.

He slipped an arm casually about her. Her pulse rate quickened at the reminder of the way things had once been between them. This, she thought, was a parody—a practised ploy to deceive an audience. But there was nothing she could do about it. Much as she disliked being held so close to him, Brooke had to admit that the support was welcome. She was exhausted. They had been so busy that the carnival had been harder work than she had expected. That, plus the emotional strain that she'd been under for the last three days, had left her about to collapse.

Late afternoon shadows were beginning to fall across the park, and the heat of the day was slowly dissipating. Brooke shivered, and wasn't sure if it was because of the cooling air or because of the muscled arm strong about her.

In the bandstand at the corner of the park, chairs were being set up for a concert that night. Already several members of the band had taken their seats and were warming up. Some of the carnival-goers were drifting towards the bandstand, spreading blankets on the grass or setting up lawn chairs, ready for the music to start. Children had left the carnival games for the playground in the far corner of the huge square.

A strange feeling of having done it all before swept over Brooke. She and Ty had come to the band concerts every week, that summer of their engagement. They had always spread a blanket in the shadows to sit on, and they had watched the sun set behind the library, and held hands, and listened to the music. And after the band had finished, and the crowd had gone home, Brooke and Ty had stayed and snuggled together in the blanket as the dusk spun itself into warm night . . .

She had not come to a band concert since. She hadn't even been aware, until now, that she had purposely avoided these small-town evenings in the park. She hadn't acknowledged that events like this reminded her too much of Ty.

Just where was he taking her? she wondered abruptly. He had told her a few minutes ago that he would prefer privacy when it was time to collect the kiss that she still owed him. She'd almost forgotten about that. She wondered, with momentary panic, if he was taking her up to his hotel suite. And, if he was, what if he didn't intend to stop with a kiss at all?

But they merely walked past the hotel, and Brooke tried to conceal her sigh of relief.

'I'll drive you up to Oakley if you like,' he said. 'But if you're not too tired, let's walk. We do need to decide on a few things. Setting a wedding date, for example.'

Brooke shrugged. 'It couldn't matter less to me,' she said with airy unconcern.

'Then we'll be married next Saturday.' His tone was cool.

She tried to pull away from him. 'Next Saturday? You must be crazy!'

'You said a moment ago that it didn't matter,' he reminded her gently. He tucked her hand into his elbow, and held her securely against his side.

'But surely not that soon! I thought——' Her tongue was stumbling over itself as she begged. 'In the autumn——'

'There's a limit to how much I'll advance Emily until after the wedding.'

'Don't you trust me to keep my word?' she asked bitterly.

'Of course I trust the word of a Carlisle.' Ty's words had an ironic twist. 'But sometimes strange things happen, Brooke. We found that out the last time we were engaged. This time you'll get no opportunity to change your mind.'

She bit her tongue, determined not to retaliate, as she certainly could have, by saying something about his behaviour. What was the point? She certainly didn't want to invite him to tell whatever story he had thought up to explain why he had been kissing Alison in the solarium that day. It was over and done with. Why bring it up again?

'The wedding will be on Saturday,' he repeated blandly.

Brooke refused to look at him or to acknowledge the order.

'Just in case I didn't make myself clear,' he added, 'I want you to know that this will not be simply a marriage of convenience, or appearance, or whatever you might want to call it. I have every intention of sharing your bed.'

She stumbled over a crack in the pavement, and his arm was suddenly a bulwark to steady her. She forced her voice to remain steady, casual. 'I assumed that was what you meant.'

'Good. I'm glad we understand each other.' There was a brief silence, then he added, 'I must say I'm amazed that you don't have anything further to say about it.'

Brooke looked up at him, pretending astonishment. 'Oh—do you mean that you care how I feel about sleeping with you? That's certainly the first time you've shown any concern about my feelings.'

His eyes had darkened with irritation, but she went on blindly. 'Or did you expect me to throw myself at your feet and beg you to make love to me? We old-maid librarians don't get many flattering offers like yours, you know!'

Ty threw his head back and laughed. It amazed her, and then made her furious, that he wasn't taking her seriously. He seemed to expect that as a matter of course she would be eager to share his bed and his favours. He was a cold-blooded, conceited, arrogant swine, she told herself, to think that mere physical desire could take the place of caring, of affection, of love!

'Are you?' he said suddenly. 'I've been curious.'

She was confused. 'Am I what?'

'A novel lover, as your T-shirt says.'

She hesitated. Would he even believe her? she wondered. From some of the things he had said earlier, he had long ago written her off as some kind of tramp. Very softly, she told the truth. 'I don't know.'

He didn't answer, but she knew by the way he looked down at her that he was pleased. Damn, she thought. I should have told him I'd had a hundred lovers!

Then she thought better of it. It wouldn't have disturbed him anyway, she thought; he would simply have shrugged his shoulders and warned her not to take any in the future.

Just let me get Emily through school, she thought, and Tara and I can make it on our own. Then I'll tell Ty Marshall what I really think of him! That will be my revenge. I'll use him for my own purposes, and then I'll walk away and laugh at him.

Seven years, she reminded herself, until Emily finished college. Seven long years stretched out like a bleak, endless winter before her. In the meantime, she thought, she could always hope that Emily would change her mind about doing law.

'We should have a quiet wedding,' he said, as if to himself. 'A big one would be in bad taste, I think, without your father to give you away.'

The lump in her throat threatened to choke her. My God, how much I miss him, she thought. If Dad were here none of this would be happening to me. He wouldn't let it.

'A simple ceremony, of course. If you need any financial help for the arrangements . . . '

'I assure you that I have no intention of going into debt over this fiasco.'

'A white dress, at least, would be nice.' Ty looked down at her in the gathering twilight, speculatively.

They had never got as far as planning their wedding before. It would have been a whole year away, anyway, and there had been more important things to talk about. But there would have been certain standards to keep up.

My wedding would have been the social event of the season, Brooke thought. Sarcasm sharpened her voice. 'White satin, I suppose, with a train? And orange blossom? And a champagne fountain?' she demanded. 'Come on, Ty. Let's not make this any more of a joke than it has to be!'

'You know just how to pull off a simple wedding with style, I'm sure,' he said. 'Whether you will do it is, of course, a different question.'

'What do you mean by that?'

'We'll see just how deep your elegant surface goes, Miss

Carlisle,' he said. 'I'm betting you have a vulgar streak that you won't be able to keep hidden, because of your desire to embarrass me by showing up in red taffeta and feathers, or something of the sort.'

She tried to look thoughtful, as if the idea had just struck her. 'It would be a great deal of fun.'

'Oh, you can make me look a fool, if you like,' he admitted comfortably, 'but only by throwing your own public image down the drain as well. And you may find that I don't embarrass all that easily. Yes,' he added thoughtfully, 'it should be interesting to see what sort of wedding you'll arrange.'

The blandness of his voice left Brooke speechless. They strolled up the drive towards Oakley, its windows gleaming red and gold in the last rays of sunlight. To an observer, she thought, they would have looked like lovers, her hand confidently on his arm as they walked so close together.

'Tyler . . . ' she said at last.

'Yes, my dear?' The words were gentle, but the tone was matter-of-fact, more an expression of ownership than of tenderness.

Tears threatened her. She stopped in the centre of the driveway. 'Tyler,' she said again. 'You told me once, long ago, that you loved me. I beg you, for the sake of that affection, not to do this to me now.'

He frowned. 'I thought you realised that affection has nothing to do with it, Brooke.'

She swallowed the lump in her throat. Yes, I know, she thought. But I was hoping that somewhere, deep in your heart, you still cherished a tiny bit of fondness for me . . .

He seemed to read her mind. 'I adored you, Brooke. You represented everything that had been lacking in my life—the beauty, the graciousness, the ease of living——'

'The money, the business, the house,' she added bitterly.

'Those too,' he admitted without shame.

'But now that I don't have those things any more——'

'You have the ones that matter,' he said. 'And I'm quite willing to supply the rest in exchange.' He looked up at the peaks of Oakley's roof, where sunshine still played against the rough brick. 'I've always wanted to be the master of Oakley Manor,' he mused.

'Will nothing change your mind?' she said, under her breath.

'Nothing.'

At the front door, he stopped and released her hand. 'I won't come in,' he said.

'You weren't invited,' Brooke pointed out.

The last rays of sunlight caught and glistened on his silver hair. One lock of it was wind-ruffled; she almost reached up to smooth it before she caught herself.

'I'll stop by the library tomorrow,' said Ty. 'We'll have to go and see the pastor very soon, of course.'

'He won't marry us, you know,' said Brooke. 'Not at six days' notice. He's very particular about that.'

Ty smiled. 'My darling, where did you get the idea that he'll only have six days' notice?'

She stamped her foot, wishing it was him she was stepping on instead of the stone paving. 'Did everyone in the world know about this stupid wedding before I did?' she accused.

'You didn't seem to want to hear the details,' Ty said, with mock apology.'And speaking of details . . . ' He reached into his pocket, 'I'm glad I won't have to carry this around any more.'

She folded her arms, refusing even to look at the tiny box he held out, much less to reach for it. With a half-smile, Ty opened the box and waved an engagement ring under her nose.

Against the white velvet lining, a huge emerald winked like an evil eye. It must have been two carats in size. Surrounding it was a host of baguette diamonds, pieced together as precisely as the bits of a jigsaw puzzle, in a ballerina setting that added sparkle to the clear deep green of the emerald. 'It's a little nicer than the last one I gave you,' he murmured. 'It should be less embarrassing for you to be seen wearing this one.'

'Oh, hell,' muttered Brooke.

What a lovely thing to say about a ring,' he said agreeably. 'It will make a fascinating story to tell the children, around the fireplace on some cold winter night.'

'Children?' she echoed. Her voice had a breathless catch in it.

'Yes. You don't think I was doing this only for myself, did you? I want my kids to have the best. They won't grow up as outcasts, as I did.'

Brooke swallowed hard. 'But——'

'I'm sorry if the ring isn't the right size. The jeweller took a guess, but you may have to return it to be altered.' He slid the emerald firmly on to her finger; then raised her hand to his lips. 'You owe me a kiss,' he mused. 'But I think I'll wait and let it collect a little interest first. See you tomorrow.'

He sauntered off into the dusk, whistling. Brooke stood on the steps with her hands clenched together, the emerald cutting a pattern into her skin, and watched him go.

Children, she thought. Well, he'd be disillusioned about that soon enough. He couldn't force her to give him a child. She thought about the possibility of a small person with Ty's charming, determined and difficult nature, and shuddered. Children! The very idea! He ought to know better than to think she'd go along with that.

The house was quiet, but she followed the murmur of the stereo into the living-room. Tara was lying on one of the long couches, covered with a blanket. Her face was red and she had obviously been crying. Beside her the coffee-table was drawn up close, and a glass of ginger ale bubbled on the corner of it.

Brooke stopped in the doorway. 'Oh, no!' she exclaimed. 'What's this?'

Emily looked up from her magazine. 'She has a stomach ache.'

'Too many chilli dogs?'

'Not any more,' Emily said cheerfully. 'She got rid of those a few minutes ago. Now she's no longer at death's door, she's just miserable.'

Tara opened her eyes. 'Brooke,' she said. 'I wanted you, and you weren't here!'

'I'm here now, darling.' The child's head was hot to Brooke's touch.

'Well, how's that for thanks!' grumbled Emily. 'I'm here to hold her hand, but she wants you. Tara the Terrible does it again. She's running half a degree of fever, by the way.'

'Is that all? She feels as if she's burning up.' Brooke tucked Tara's blanket in again.

'My God!' Emily exclaimed. 'What's that thing on your finger?' She seized Brooke's hand and inspected the emerald in its ballerina setting. Then she looked up at her sister with delight in her eyes. 'The guy has class, that's for sure. I've never seen anything so pretty. Lucky girl!'

That's what everybody keeps telling me, Brooke thought. 'What are you reading?' she asked.

Emily grinned. 'I stopped and got all the bridal magazines,' she confided. 'I thought we'd better get started planning.'

'Well, let me know what you decide,' said Brooke. 'The wedding is next weekend.'

The magazines slid off Emily's lap. Her mouth had dropped open. 'But what are you going to wear? There won't be time to order a dress!'

Black bombazine with a hangman's noose sounds appropriate to me, thought Brooke bitterly. 'We'll just have to make do.'

'But you only get married once! You can't just settle for second best.'

Why not? Brooke thought. I'm certainly getting no prize for a husband!

'This is the most important day of your life,' Emily went on. 'Ty will just have to be patient for a few more months.'

'So why don't you talk to him about putting it off?' Brooke suggested sweetly.

'He'll have to wait a few weeks at least. It's just not possible that we can be ready by the weekend.' Emily shook her head definitely.

'What is there to do?' asked Brooke. 'It won't take any time to get ready. I've got that pale blue dress I bought for the club dance last autumn. Ty's already arranged for the church, and I suppose he'll provide me with a corsage.

What else do we need? I'm sure you wouldn't mind being a witness. He can find the other one himself.'

Emily flung her hands out dramatically, then jumped to her feet and paced the room. 'A Carlisle?' she said. 'Getting married in an indecent hurry, in an ordinary dress, without guests, without a veil, without candles on the altar?'

Brooke shrugged. 'You can light a candle if you like. And at least I'll be wearing something old and blue.'

'Everybody will think you have something to hide. And with good reason. You make your wedding sound like something to be ashamed of! I'll be right back.' Emily stormed out of the room.

Well, Brooke thought, Emily was right about that. And perhaps she had a point; it wouldn't take long for the gossip to spread that the new Mrs Tyler Marshall hadn't been terribly excited about her marriage.

Tara sat up with a groan. 'Brooke, are you really getting married? Emily said so, but I thought she was teasing me!'

'Yes, darling.'

Tara's face crumpled, and she started to sob.

Brooke knelt beside the couch. 'Honey, you mustn't cry!' she pleaded. 'You'll just make the stomach ache worse. Please, Tara!'

The child's sobs grew even stronger.

Oh, no, Brooke thought. Of all the things I don't need tonight, a child in hysterics is at the top of the list. 'But I thought you liked Mr Marshall!'

Emily came back into the room and cast herself down like a rag doll into her chair. 'I just talked to Ty,' she announced. 'The wedding will be Saturday.'

Tara started to wail anew.

'Well, I didn't think you'd have any luck,' said Brooke drily. She stroked Tara's hair, murmured soothing words into her ear, and when the sobs had died to hiccups, helped her to take a sip of ginger ale.

Emily was staring into the empty fireplace, as if brooding. Then she seemed to pull herself together. 'There's no reason why it can't be classy,' she said, 'even if Ty is in an indecent hurry. After all, you can only have a white wedding once.'

Classy, thought Brooke. Tyler had said something about that, too. Since childhood she had dreamed about the wedding she wanted. Why should she be cheated of everything, even if this wasn't precisely the way she would have chosen to be married? Emily was right about it being one day in a lifetime. Even if some day she was free of Ty—which she was beginning to doubt—and she married again, etiquette said she could never have the long gown and veil, the big reception, the wedding dance that she had long dreamed of.

Most of that was mere silliness anyway, she thought. A person was just as much married with a simple ceremony as one that included a whole day of celebrating. But there were certain things that she would like to have.

It would please Tyler, of course. There was nothing she wanted to do less than that. On the other hand, if she gave up the things she wanted just to spite him, she too would be unhappy.

She patted Tara's shoulder absentmindedly. 'Tara, you must cut out this nonsense, or you'll be sick for a week.'

'I don't care,' Tara sniffed.

'But you will care. You'll miss your class picnic.'

Emily had vanished again. She's up to something, Brooke thought, then put it out of her mind. 'All right, Tara,' she said firmly. 'You're big enough to know that your stomach hurts only because you ate too many chilli dogs. You also know you'll feel much better tomorrow, if you'll only stop feeling sorry for yourself. So what are you really crying about?'

Tara stuck her bottom lip out stubbornly.

'If you don't want to tell me about it, you don't have to,' Brooke told her. 'But problems don't get better until you talk them over. Emily, what are you up to now?'

'Inspiration,' the girl said. She was carrying a large brown dress box. 'Didn't you tell me once that Mom put this away for us to wear?'

The very thought sent shivers down Brooke's spine. She had forgotten her mother's wedding gown. Could she bear to disgrace an heirloom by wearing it to marry Ty Marshall in the blackmail match of the century?

Emily put the box down reverently in the centre of the carpet. Even Tara sat up to watch as she opened the box.

Brooke remembered seeing the dress once. She'd been in the attic with her mother, and had asked what was in the big box. Her mother had opened it carefully, and told her that it was put away for Brooke's wedding day, and Emily's. It had been long before Tara was born.

But Brooke had been so little herself that she remembered almost nothing about the dress. She'd looked at it a hundred times in her parents' stiffly formal wedding portrait, of course, but she still couldn't deny a little thrill of anticipation as Emily carefully unfolded the crackly blue tissue paper.

Emily sat back on her heels with a long sigh. Tara craned her neck. Brooke reached out with a tentative finger to touch the delicate fabric, ivory with age.

The satin wasn't even creased, so carefully had it been layered with tissue. Overlaying the bodice and trailing down here and there over the skirt was delicate lace, aged now to an even deeper tone of ivory than the satin. It was a simple but elegant dress, more tailored than frilly.

'The picture didn't do it justice,' said Brooke.

'That's an understatement.' Emily lifted the dress out of the box. 'It's not quite my thing, of course—I long for ruffles and hoop-skirts. But, Brooke, it will be gorgeous on you.'

'It would fall apart if we tried to clean it.'

'No, it won't. It's not that old. Come on, let's see if it fits.'

As if hypnotised, Brooke got to her feet. Emily was already in the arched doorway on her way to the stairs with the mass of satin in her arms when Tara flopped back on the couch and wailed, 'Don't leave me alone!'

Emily snapped, 'Look, Terrible, we're only going upstairs. You won't die if you're left here by yourself for a couple of minutes——'

'Don't yell at her, Emily.' Brooke returned to the couch, sat down on the end of it by Tara's feet, and said, 'All right, Tara, don't give me any more nonsense. What's the problem?'

Tara gulped and wailed, 'Everybody's leaving me. Emmy's going to college, and you're getting married. What's going to happen to me?'

There was a moment of total silence.

'Nobody's going to love me any more,' Tara whimpered. She sounded heartbroken. 'You'll have babies to love.'

'Not for a long time,' muttered Brooke. 'And in any case, I won't love you less.' She scooped the child up into her arms.

Emily sniffed, draped the wedding dress across a high-backed chair, announced, 'You're a real little idiot, Tara,' and left the room.

It took the better part of an hour to soothe Tara to sleep. I should have seen it coming, Brooke thought. Tara never behaves like that, even when she's sick. The stomach ache and the emotional upset, put together, had added up to one very difficult little girl.

She sat there quietly, holding the sleeping child in her arms, and looked across the room at her mother's wedding gown. I wouldn't dare wear it, she thought. I'd be struck down by lightning on my way to church!

Which, she reflected, would at least mean that she would escape from Ty.

She could be petty and vindictive and make sure that they had a wedding no one in Oakley Mills would ever be able to forget. Or she could let Ty believe she had given in to his requests, and have a pleasant, simple ceremony.

From across the room, the ivory dress seemed to beckon. No matter whom she married, it seemed to be saying, her mother would have wanted her to have a pretty wedding. Besides that, there was Emily, who would never understand anything less.

Brooke lost herself in pleasant thought for a few moments, dreaming of the wedding she would have liked to have, the wedding she and Ty might have had all those years ago. But she found that it wasn't flowers and candles and dresses and cakes that came into her mind, but the look in the eyes of her man as she walked down the aisle to meet him. That was all that mattered; all the rest was mere show.

Well, she told herself grimly, that special look would never be in Tyler's eyes. It was the one thing she couldn't have. Affection doesn't enter into this arrangement, he had said—much less love. So all that was left to her was the show to soothe her pride. At least it would be something to remember, in the long years ahead.

CHAPTER EIGHT

EVERYONE in Oakley Mills agreed that despite the unusual
haste, it was a lovely wedding. All the ordinary things
happened. The bride's youngest sister scattered rose petals
over the white carpet with abandon and ran out before
she was halfway down the aisle. The bride's other sister
was serious and thoughtful and half-sick before the ceremony for fear she'd fall over her own feet as maid of
honour. They both looked quite charming in dark green
with flowers in their hair, while the bride was the most
beautiful ever in her mother's ivory satin and lace, with
her fair hair upswept and her green eyes mysteriously
shadowed. The soloist warbled all the usual verses, and
the reception starred a large, magnificent cake, but no
champagne fountain.

The bridegroom was the perfect host, calm, smiling,
and perfectly at ease. That he was neither nervous nor
deliriously happy was only logical, for he was older than
average, and could hardly be expected to react as a
younger man would. And if the bride seemed a bit quiet
and pale—well, that was something to be remarked on! It
was rare these days—yes, and rather sweet, too—to see a
bride who was still just a bit shy with her new husband.

Yes, agreed the guests, these two fully understood the
seriousness of the step they was taking. Oh, not that they
weren't in love! Why, you could see that in a minute, just
by the way they looked today! But you could also tell
that they meant this to last—for better, for worse, and
for ever.

And if anyone had a chance at a solid marriage, surely
it was Tyler and Brooke, the guests decided. They had
everything going for them—money, position, a solid background, a lot of interests in common. How wonderful it

was that they were going to stay in Oakley Mills! Of
course, you'd have a hard time convincing the Carlisles
to leave Oakley Manor. But to think that this man was
willing to take on the old plant's problems, simply because
his bride wanted to live here! How delightful it was to see
a young couple so willing to compromise!

If a few of the guests noticed that Dave Sheridan had
come to the church late, sat in a back pew, and muttered
to himself at the reception, there was sympathy and not
censure in their comments. Dave was a nice guy, they
agreed, but everyone knew that he just wasn't quite right
for Brooke Carlisle. Of course, until Ty Marshall had
come back to town, it had looked as if Dave and Brooke
would end up together. But as soon as Tyler appeared on
the scene, it had become obvious, one of the women said.
She had seen Ty and Brooke together several times in
those first few days he had been in town, she claimed,
and it was apparent from the outset that they still had
strong feelings about each other.

Of course, others said. Why, they'd even been engaged
once before. Wasn't it wonderful that they'd come back
together again!

It was too bad, they all agreed, that Elliot hadn't lived
to give his eldest daughter away today. He'd have been
so proud of her. And it was a little surprising, some noted,
that Alison Carlisle hadn't come to the wedding. She was
still the girls' stepmother, after all; she and Elliot had
been separated, but never divorced. Shouldn't it have
been she who was hostess at this wedding, rather than
Brooke herself?

Others among the crowd sniffed. That, they said, was
only to be expected of Alison. The one thing that could
be relied on was that Alison would take care of herself. It
was no wonder that Brooke had preferred not to bring
her stepmother into it at all. Brooke was a girl with a
clear head. She'd certainly shown good sense in choosing
Ty Marshall as a husband.

The only tiny problems that the guests could see might
be those sisters of hers. Good kids, both of them, but
kids nevertheless, and a few of the women tut-tutted at

the idea of a newly married couple saddled with that kind of responsibility. Nonsense, said their husbands. The young lady had been doing quite well on her own; now she'd have a man to help and it would be even better for all of them . . .

But the women weren't convinced. Why, they weren't even having a honeymoon, just going back to Oakley Manor! Several of the ladies had offered to take Tara for a few days, so the newlyweds could have a bit of privacy. But the bride had smilingly refused. It was important for Tara, she said, for them to be a family together as soon as possible.

And, the groom added, they could always honeymoon later in the summer. A quiet week or so at the lake, perhaps—just the two of them.

Who was to know that the very idea struck coldly into his bride's heart, as she stood there beside him smiling and greeting her guests . . .

They posed for what seemed hundreds of photographs. Even Tyler showed signs of impatience before that was over. Once, as he stood on the altar steps with one arm round Brooke, his other hand placed just so under her flowers, looking down into her eyes with an expression of adoration, he whispered, 'I'm amazed that you wanted souvenirs of this.'

'I thought it would be expected,' Brooke hissed back. 'And I told him we wanted a few pictures. Not a few thousand——'

'And smile,' the photographer said. They obediently did.

'At any rate,' said Ty with a shrug, 'we'll have something to look at on our silver anniversary.'

Twenty-five years? It seemed to stretch endlessly in front of her, a long dusty pathway to walk with never a place to rest and forget. Brooke looked up with horror in her eyes. 'Even murderers sometimes get parole,' she pointed out. Ty didn't answer.

'Now we'll do one more pose of the three sisters together,' the photographer announced, 'and then we'll be done.'

Brooke tried to hide her sigh of relief. She was happy to get away from Ty; it was darned uncomfortable to stand there in public with that casually possessive arm around her.

'Go over by the candelabrum, please, Mrs Marshall.'

Mrs Marshall. That was going to be hard on her, she thought. 'Where's Tara?' she asked.

'Here she comes,' said Emily. She fussed with Brooke's dress till each fold was displayed just right. 'She was drinking all the punch at the reception, so I made her come up here with me. Are you sure you don't want us to light out tonight?' she added in a whisper.

'I'm sure.' Brooke smiled down at Tara, who had reached up to stroke a flower in her bouquet. At least Tara had calmed down, she thought. It was amazing what a little reassurance could do for a nine-year-old. A shame, she added to herself, that it wouldn't work the same wonders for a new bride, who was looking to her future with something less than anticipation.

'But Brooke—for gosh sakes, it's your wedding night! It's positively indecent not to want to be rid of us. And Jane said we could come to her apartment——'

'You're not going, Emily. And it is not indecent.'

'All right, all right. I think you're crazy to have us around, when it's your first chance to be really alone with Ty. But I won't argue any more. I'll keep Tara on a leash so she won't bother you.'

Tara could spend the night sitting on the foot of my bed and it wouldn't bother me in the slightest, thought Brooke, as long as it kept Ty away from me . . .

'That's all, ladies. Thank you for your co-operation,' said the photographer.

'Whew!' Emily sighed. 'I'm glad that's over. If you don't need us, I think I'll take the kid home. I'm a little concerned about a repeat of the chilli dog incident. She's drunk enough punch today to sink a battleship.'

'If you think it best, Em. I'm sorry about you missing the rest of the party.'

Emily shrugged. 'No offence, love, but it's not quite my kind of party.' She gave Brooke a hug. 'Go dance with your husband, and don't give a thought to Tara and me. All my best, you know, and all that. I'm happy you found him again—he's a wonderful guy. Don't let go of him this time.'

The worst thing about it, thought Brooke, was that Emily was absolutely sincere. And so were the others who had warmly given her their best wishes today. They all thought Tyler was some kind of prize.

Endurance, she thought, as she went back to her guests, her hand on Tyler's arm. That's the key. This, too, shall pass, and I won't have to hear all this silliness any more.

Eventually, it was over, and they were free to leave. 'Not having a honeymoon was a serious mistake,' Ty mused as they got into his car.

Brooke froze. 'Why?' she asked, and instantly wished she had ignored him.

'Because then we'd have had an excuse to leave hours ago. Without all this stuff.' He gestured to the back seat, packed with gifts that had been brought to the church.

So it had bothered him too, she thought. All the flowery compliments and the elaborate gifts, to honour a day that was a sham!

'It did seem a waste of time,' she said. She lost herself in contemplation of the severely plain gold band next to the huge emerald on her left hand. Such a lot of bother, she thought, for such a tiny thing.

There was a pang of longing, deep inside her, for the way it could have been. The tiny chip of a diamond, next to a thin gold band slipped on to her finger with love, instead of cold calculation . . .

He never loved me, she told herself firmly. And I never loved him. It was all a mistake. I was too young to know the difference between love and mere sexual desire. And Ty had admitted that his motives in marrying her were not much different now than they had been four years ago, just clearer.

Evening had come, and the gentle twilight was like a warm cloud hovering over the town. At Oakley, every outside light was ablaze, flooding the lawn and the house with warm welcome. Emily's touch, Brooke thought. The girl really was a sweetheart. It was too bad that her helpfulness was misplaced.

The garage door was open, and her own small car was parked at the side of the house where Emily had left it. 'We can lock your car in the garage,' Brooke suggested, 'and unload it tomorrow.'

'And leave yours out?'

'There's supposed to be room for two,' she said, 'but since we've only had one car, the other side has gotten sort of junky in the last few months. There just wasn't time to clean it out this week——'

Ty turned to her. There was a flash of irritation in his eyes, but his words were gentle. 'Don't apologise,' he said. 'You've had more than you could handle alone since your father got sick. Don't be ashamed of the job you've done.'

Brooke swallowed hard and blinked back tears. You're turning into a mushy fool, she accused herself, ready to sob because he had uttered a kind word!

Oakley, despite the blaze of lights, was quiet. The kitchen table was stacked with boxes, some that Emily had brought home from the church, others that had been delivered to the house throughout the week. On top of the pile was an envelope, addressed to them in Emily's unmistakable handwriting.

'Your dinner is in the oven and the refrigerator,' the note inside said. 'Tara and I would wait table, but we thought you'd rather be alone. We're having a bunk party in the playroom tonight. See you in the morning.'

Brooke's eyes filled with tears again. Sweet, misguided Emily, she thought, was very determined that they should have their privacy. The playroom was above the garage, as far as it was possible to get from Brooke's bedroom. She handed the note to Ty. 'You have a fan there,' she said.

'Well, one out of three isn't bad.' He yanked his bow-tie off, released the top button of his shirt, and said, 'Ties should be outlawed by the Supreme Court as cruel and unusual punishment.'

'I think Tara will come around, too,' Brooke added. 'She thought you were pretty nice until you threatened to upset her ordered life. As soon as she realises that nothing much has changed, she'll be fine.'

'Which leaves one of the three Carlisle sisters to be convinced that her lot in life has improved.'

Brooke picked up a crystal sweet dish and turned it over in her hand, inspecting the deep grooves of its pattern. 'Well, that's somewhat different.'

'Yes, I see it is.' His tone was even.

She set the dish down and went to peep into the oven. A casserole dish steamed gently, sending out the scent of chicken. In the refrigerator were two elaborate salads. No wonder Emily had ducked out of the reception early, Brooke thought. She had been busy.

'I'm going up to change my clothes,' she said finally. 'I'd hate to spill something on Mother's dress.'

That got Ty's attention. 'I didn't realise it was hers.' There was a warm glow in his eyes. 'I just knew that you looked beautiful in it.'

Suddenly she was defensive, which was silly. Whose business was it, anyway, what she chose to wear? If Ty was silly enough to think that wearing her mother's dress meant that she had come to terms with the idea of marrying him, she couldn't stop him. What did it matter what he thought?

But it did matter. She had to make him understand, somehow. 'Ty,' she said. 'We have some things to talk about. I don't feel quite right about discussing them in the kitchen. Would you come with me?'

'Of course, my dear.'

She led the way through the dining-room, where the table was laid neatly with her mother's best china and silver. Candles stood ready to light, and at the two places were hors d'oeuvre, already in place—small bowls of mixed fruit, each set into a larger one of crushed ice. Not precisely according to the rules, but it was ingenious of Emily none the less, Brooke thought. On the sideboard a bottle of champagne was cooling in an ice bucket. Just where, she wondered, had Emily come up with that? She certainly wasn't old enough to buy it!

Brooke gave up wondering about her resourceful

younger sister and led the way down the hall. She hurried
up the stairs, trying not to lose her nerve. If she stopped
to think about it, she'd back out, and it was vital that
they have this little chat. It was very important that Ty
be made to understand precisely how she felt, and what
restrictions she was putting on this little game.

'Are you eager for us to be alone?' asked Ty. He
sounded amused. 'I'm flattered that my bride is so
anxious . . . '

Brooke pretended not to have heard.

She was surprised he didn't pause to glance around the
hallway and through the open doors. Surely he must feel
some curiosity about the private areas of this house that
he had acquired at such expense—but he seemed to know
exactly where he was going.

Perhaps Alison had brought him up here, she thought.
The master suite had been Alison's then. Bitterness washed
over Brooke. Just how far had he gone with Alison? she
wondered. In the months before their engagement, while
she had still been at school, had he carried on an affair
with her stepmother? It was bad enough to find him
kissing her, Brooke thought, but to think about him
making love to her, here, made her feel nauseated.

And now it was Brooke's bedroom. At least, she
thought, thank God it isn't the same bed. That alone
makes it worth all the work I did changing it after Alison
left.

She shut the door of her bedroom firmly behind them
and leaned against it.

'You're not exactly pleased with the idea that I'm here,'
he observed. He was looking around, as if assessing the
changes in the room. He walked across to the windows,
looked out, then closed the curtains.

'No, I'm not.' It was curt, hard. 'Two points for
accuracy.'

Tyler shrugged. 'May I suggest that you make every
effort to become accustomed to my presence? Because I
don't plan to leave Oakley, ever. I've paid too much for
it.'

'That's part of what I want to talk to you about,' she said stiffly.

He raised a dark eyebrow, patiently waiting. He was perfectly relaxed as he stood there, tall and handsome in the dark evening clothes. And despite his calm air, she was afraid of him.

'I cleared a closet for you, over there,' she said. 'And there are some empty drawers. There's a sitting-room through there——'

'I know,' he said politely.

Brooke clenched her fists. It had been Alison's dressing-room. Had he helped her out of her clothes there, like some doll, kissing her and teasing her——

'And there's a couch that pulls out into a bed,' she added fiercely, refusing even to think about him with Alison. 'You needn't increase the discomfort you feel here at Oakley by thinking you have to entertain me.'

He smiled slightly. 'If that's a polite way to tell me I shouldn't force myself to share your bed——'

'It was. I certainly wouldn't want you to think I would be disappointed.'

'Then I will once again attempt to make myself clear. To correct your mistaken impression, Brooke, I don't consider making love to you an obligation but a fringe benefit.'

Brooke swallowed hard. How could he even call it making love, she thought bitterly—to sleep with a woman he admitted no fondness for? 'If all you want is to be accepted socially, you certainly don't need to——'

He moved across the room and propped an elbow on the mantelpiece. He looked totally at ease, dominating the room. 'No,' he disagreed. 'If that was all I wanted, I'd have done it myself—the tooth and claw, time-consuming way that you so helpfully recommended that night at the club. But that wouldn't have gotten Oakley for me—or you to grace my bed.'

'I still can't believe you want to make this a real marriage,' she said sharply. 'What about love?'

'Love is an illusion, meant for children to dream of,' he said gently. 'Real life leaves no room for dreams of

that sort. We've been through all of this before, Brooke.
Either you haven't been listening, or you're hoping to
appeal to my chivalrous side with all this talk of love.
Which is it?'

She sat down on the end of the bed. She was shaking
inside. 'You haven't got a chivalrous side.'

Ty smiled, just a little. 'Now you're catching on. Isn't
it time to stop playing games, Brooke?'

There was a brief silence while she fought to get her
breath back. It was foolish, she thought, to try to argue
with him when he held all the cards.

She put out a hand to brace herself, and for the first
time noticed a sheer, lace-trimmed yellow négligé spread
out over the foot of the bed. Emily again, she concluded.
The girl must have dug deep into her savings to buy that.
Or else—knowing Emily—she had charged it to Brooke's
account . . . It hardly mattered, Brooke told herself, for
even if she ended up paying for that wisp of sexy lace,
she would never wear it.

She forced herself to stand up. Ty might rob her of her
dignity, he might force her to do as he demanded, he
might humiliate her, but he could never break her pride
unless she bowed to him. And, she was determined, she
would never bow.

'All right,' she said finally. Her voice was low and hard,
and fury was eating away at her common sense. 'You
demanded marriage—I've paid your price. If you insist
that sleeping with you is part of it, then I'll do what I
have to do.'

There was a gleam in his eyes, something that might
have been reluctant admiration, but he said nothing.

'I'll submit to you,' she went on, her words stumbling
over each other, 'if I must. So let's get it over with!'

'Oh, you'll do much more than submit to me, Brooke.
Don't forget I have a lifetime to wait, if it takes that
long.'

The words struck fear deep into her heart. 'I'll share a
bed with you, if I have to,' she cried. 'But my heart and
my mind are reserved for the man I can love.'

'You don't know what love is, any more than I do,' he

said. 'We're two of a kind, Brooke—out to get what we can. Why don't you just tell the truth? Or does it hurt too much to admit that you want me to make love to you?'

'You lousy hypocrite!' The words were out before she paused to consider that they might act as a match to paper. But she didn't care. 'All you know is lust, Ty. Only an animal can be satisfied with that——'

'Right now,' he said, 'I would find it very satisfying. Don't try my patience, Brooke.'

'That's all you'll ever have from me, Ty Marshall! You might possess my body, but you'll never have anything else!'

There was a long, dead silence, like the breathless hesitation before a storm.

'Then I have no reason to wait, do I?' he said pleasantly. 'There is obviously nothing to be gained by acting like a gentleman.' He stripped off the black tailcoat, flung it down on the loveseat by the windows and came across the room towards her. 'Shall I help you out of your dress, my dear?' His hand on her shoulder spun her around, and his fingers were cold against the nape of her neck as he started down the long row of satin-covered buttons.

She forced the panic from her voice, but it still trembled a little. 'Don't tear it,' she whispered.

'I'll try to control myself,' he said. 'Animal lust is a difficult thing to overcome, however. I'm sure you understand how it is when one is tempted by a paragon like yourself!' His voice cracked like a whip.

She shrugged out of the satin dress as soon as she could, afraid he would shred it. He picked her up bodily and flung her on to the bed. She clenched her fists on the edges of a pillow, thinking, Oh, my God, I've only made it worse. I mustn't fight him or he'll hurt me . . .

But he surprised her again, for his touch was gentle. His fingertips stroked every inch of exposed skin, a featherlight touch that tickled and tormented and sent shivers running through her body.

'Did you know, my dear,' he whispered, his mouth against her throat, 'that a woman's skin is actually the

most sensitive part of her? The gentlemen of old who used
to kiss their ladies' hands knew that.'

His lips brushed her sensitive throat, and a long shudder
ran through her. This innocent touch of his was the most
intimate she had ever been subjected to. She tried to pull
away from him.

'Are you afraid, Brooke?' he asked. 'But you told me
that you would submit to my—animal lust. Are you
already backing out on that promise?'

She forced herself to lie quietly, and tried to steady her
breathing, and Ty resumed that gentle, tortuous stroking
of her skin as he stripped her of the rest of her clothes.
She was afraid, she had to admit, but it wasn't so much
fear of him, just now, but of herself. Somewhere deep
within her there seemed to be a storm brewing, and she
was afraid that if she once lost control of it, it would be
like riding a hurricane.

She closed her eyes and tried to say her multiplication
tables, but she hadn't got through the first set when Ty
released the hooks on her bra. Then he bent his head to
her breast, and her body betrayed her. Long shivers of
pleasure rocketed through her, and a tiny moan escaped
her lips.

Ty raised his head. 'So,' he said softly. 'The lady isn't
quite as indifferent as she tries to appear.'

His mouth claimed hers, then, not harshly, but with a
demand that she give him back, bit for bit, the pleasure
that he gave—a pleasure he was only too capable of
giving, and one that she wanted so badly to receive that
every other concern was forgotten in the rising storm of
passion.

She didn't know precisely when she stopped clutching
the pillow and began clinging to him instead. She had no
idea of the exact moment when instead of merely
responding to his demands, she began to make her own.
She only knew that when he pulled away and looked
closely at her, she was hurt, bereft, lost without his touch.

'Please——' she whispered, and blindly tried to draw
him back to her.

But instead, Ty pulled further away. 'Who's a hypocrite

now?' he asked, very softly. 'That was an interesting display of animal lust in the female of the species, my dear.'

She thought, vaguely, that his voice was shaky. But that wasn't possible, she told herself. He had done this on purpose, cold and calculated, to make a fool of her. It hadn't meant a thing to him.

'At least,' he added, 'I assume that you're not going to try to convince me that you've fallen in love with me in the last fifteen minutes.' He raked a hand through his hair, and rolled off the bed. 'So Brooke has purely physical reactions, too,' he said, and flung the négligé at her.

Why should I bother to put it on? she thought. He's certainly seen everything there is to see. 'You're not going to——' she started, hesitantly. Her tongue seemed to stumble over the words.

'No, I'm not going to gratify you, and let you cry rape in the morning. I did intend to make love to you tonight, and you would have enjoyed it. But you certainly have an effective way of killing desire.' His tone was harsh.

Brooke pulled the négligé on, haphazardly. She was still lying across the crumpled bedspread, and she felt too weak to move at all. She should be glad, she thought. She had won, after all.

Ty paced across the room, and came back to stand at the foot of the bed, staring down at her. 'What in the hell is it,' he said, with fury burning through his voice, 'that makes you think you possess what it takes to drive men mad for you?'

'I don't know what you mean——'

'Of course you do. You seemed to think that because I was alone in a room with you I'd be unable to control my baser desires. Well, personally, Brooke, I've always preferred my women willing. I've never been intrigued by pretty princesses who think they needn't even be pleasant to the lesser creatures of the earth.'

'Get out!' she cried.

'My pleasure. Sleep well, pretty Brooke.'

The sitting-room door slammed behind him.

Brooke buried her head in her pillow. Sobs tore at her throat, tears of rage and anger and humiliation, and frustration because he had refused to fulfil that strange desire he had so thoroughly aroused in her.

'I hate him,' she told herself. 'I hate what he did to me!' And he had walked away, seemingly untouched.

What had he said about her? A pretty princess, not even pleasant to those around her. 'He's wrong,' she said, but there was less than certainty in her voice. The things she had said to him, and about him . . . The accusations she had flung at him . . .

Tomorrow I'll sort it all out, she thought. She crept off the bed and reached into the drawer where she always kept her nightgowns, then thought, what does it matter? One thing was certain, she told herself, and that was that the attraction she held for Ty was obviously not of the overpowering sort. He'd made that perfectly obvious. She might as well wear the yellow négligé; it would at least please Emily. Some wedding night, she thought.

She pulled the covers back and slid into bed. She was so tired and so near the brink of hysteria that for a moment she was honestly puzzled about why her feet wouldn't go completely under the blankets.

Then it dawned on her. Precious, sweet, thoughtful Emily, her lovable little sister, had short-sheeted her bed.

CHAPTER NINE

BROOKE was nearly always the first one up in the morning; she enjoyed her early walks and the quiet of Oakley while Emily and Tara still slept. But she woke up on the morning after her wedding to the vague knowledge of someone else's presence in the room, and lay pretending to be asleep as Tyler quietly unpacked and settled his belongings in the chest of drawers.

He had brought one large suitcase up to Oakley the day before the wedding. One large suitcase, and he had moved into her life and taken over her house as thoroughly as if he had arrived in a removal van. And he obviously intended to stay.

I thought it was going to be so easy, she told herself wryly. What was I giving up by marrying him, anyway, compared to the horrible possibility of selling Oakley?

But Ty had taught her, last night, that there were worse things than marrying a man she didn't love. One of them was to find herself longing for the man's touch, whimpering like a rejected pet because he didn't want her after all, and knowing that if he had stayed with her she would have given him every response a husband could desire.

She opened her eyes cautiously. His back was turned to her. He hadn't put on his shirt yet, and she lay there and watched him as he efficiently transferred clothes from suitcase to drawers. His hair gleamed silver in the sunlight, and she tried to remember if she had actually stroked it last night or if she had merely wanted to. She must have done it, she thought, for she knew that it was even softer than she had remembered, almost silky against her fingers.

She had seen him shirtless before, of course, all those years ago. She had always known he was strong, but she had never pictured the muscles shifting and turning under his brown skin, making her want to reach out and touch him and draw him down to her again . . .

Stop it, she told herself fiercely. She had never been so ashamed of herself in all her life, or so puzzled by her own rampaging thoughts. She felt strange this morning, as if a different woman had awakened inside her body, a woman who was sensual and abandoned and erotic—a woman who wanted to know what would have happened to her had Ty not left her bed last night.

He picked up his shirt, and a tiny reluctant sigh escaped her. She caught herself too late to stop it, and instantly closed her eyes, trying to keep her breathing slow and steady. She could almost feel him watching her, and the moments seemed to stretch out for ever. But finally, the door clicked shut behind him, and his footsteps faded down the hall.

It was utterly stupid to feel as if there was anything so astounding about the way she had responded to him, she told herself fiercely, trying to make herself believe it. She pushed the blankets back, too impatient with herself to stay in bed.

There was nothing so unusual about it, she decided. It was just that she was no longer an inexperienced teenager, holding back, just a little afraid of the power of the man she cared for. That was all that had changed. Never once had she relaxed her control like that when she had been with any other man. If she had, she told herself, she would have discovered the same reactions, the same nervous anticipation she had felt last night. It hadn't been the man who was responsible for that violent reaction but Brooke herself. She was sure of it. Deep inside her had been hiding a sexual hunger she had never anticipated. It had taken her by surprise, and she had lost all sense. But it was only coincidence that it had been in Ty's arms that she had made that shattering discovery.

'So,' she lectured herself as she took a shower, 'you stay away from Ty, and you'll have no more trouble.'

He was in the kitchen when she came down. She hesitated in the hallway for a moment to brace herself for what was certain to be an embarrassing meeting. Then she glanced into the dining-room and for the first time remembered the elegant supper that Emily had prepared for them.

The strawberries had sunk into purplish mush, the peach slices had turned sickly brown, and the melon balls had wilted as the crushed ice had melted away. Brooke smothered a sigh and carried them out to the kitchen. At least, she thought, Emily hadn't seen that her work had been wasted.

Tyler was pouring pancake batter on to the griddle when she came in. He didn't even look up. Bacon was sizzling in the microwave, and the aroma of coffee was beginning to fill the room.

'I hope you don't mind me making myself at home,' he said.

Brooke shrugged. 'It's fine with me. It smells very good.'

'I was hungry,' he admitted.

Brooke didn't look at him. She didn't dare remind herself of why they hadn't eaten the night before.

'You have a very well-organised kitchen,' Ty added. 'I found almost everything I needed on first try.'

She dumped the fruit down the garbage disposal, rinsed the bowls, and put them in the dishwasher. She was fighting to keep her composure; the one thing she had not expected from him this morning was a compliment! But it was almost as if they had made a silent agreement to pretend that the events of the previous night had never happened.

'Emily's the one with the logical mind,' she said finally.

'I hope I didn't disturb you this morning.' For the first time he turned to look at her.

Brooke stared directly at him and told what she was certain would be only the first whopper of the day. 'I didn't even realise you were up.' She opened the oven to get Emily's casserole out. Down the garbage disposal with that, too, she thought, before Emily had a chance to see her creation burned and dried out from being left there to warm all night. But the casserole dish was gone. She checked the refrigerator and found it there, covered with foil. It didn't look too bad after all, she thought. Ty must have taken care of it this morning.

She stirred the chicken and pasta together, trying to make it look as if a couple of servings had been removed. It didn't look quite convincing, she thought, but perhaps they could spin Emily a yarn about not having been very hungry last night. At least it would be less embarrassing than the truth.

Ty was piling pancakes on to two plates. Brooke got mats and silver out and put them on a tray to carry into the dining-room. 'I'll set the table,' she said. 'And then I'll tackle that pile of boxes after breakfast, so we can get back to normal.' She glanced at the haphazard pile of wedding gifts and sighed. What a way to spend a Sunday! And there were more still out in Ty's car. He'd be anxious to get those unloaded . . .

'Don't bother, unless you want to do it,' he said. 'Mrs Wilson can take care of it tomorrow.'

She stopped in the kitchen doorway. 'I don't have Mrs Wilson any more. I had to give her up last autumn.'

'I know. Emily told me. She'll start to work again in the morning.' He wasn't looking at her, but he seemed to feel her hesitation. 'Consider her a wedding present.'

Tears prickled in the corners of her eyes. He was being so damned kind that she would just like to throw something at him, she thought. After the way she had treated him, and the things she had said to him, for him to behave like this was more than she could bear.

And that, she told herself, was probably exactly what he had in mind!

The pancakes were good. Brooke cleaned her plate in silence.

'Another cup of coffee?' asked Ty. She nodded, and he went to the kitchen for the pot.

I have to break this silence, she thought. It's silly, and it's going to be obvious to the girls that something isn't right. We have to at least talk to each other!

'Thank you for Mrs Wilson,' she said at last. 'I've missed her.'

'I'm sure she'll be a trial for you for the first couple of

weeks, until she gets the house back precisely as she likes it.'

Brooke smiled. 'That's true. Oakley was her pride and joy.'

'Just ignore her. Actually, the house looks wonderful, considering how little time you've had to keep it up.' He sipped his coffee. 'As long as we're talking about your job, Brooke——'

Her eyes widened. That was something she had never considered. It was partial freedom for her, she realised. Would he insist that she give up her work?

'Do you want me to quit?' she asked.

'That's entirely up to you. But I want you to understand that all of Oakley's expenses are mine, now. If you work, your salary is yours to do whatever you like with.'

'Including running away from home?' she asked, and instantly regretted the flippancy.

He didn't laugh. His eyes were dark grey as he answered, 'If you want. But remember this, Brooke. I can't stop you from going, but you will leave Oakley behind as well as me. I'm not giving it up, and I'm not leaving.'

She stared down at her empty plate. She'd done it again, she saw—she had given him yet another illustration of her holier-than-thou attitude. He must have quite a collection of them by now, she thought.

She considered telling him that she had no intention of going away, that she had made up her mind to make the best of life with him. Besides, she thought, if she left, she would sacrifice everything she had married him for—Emily's college fund and Oakley. She might gain a bit of freedom, but at an even higher cost than she would have paid last week, before the wedding ring had been placed so firmly on her finger.

But he didn't seem to expect an answer, and so she said nothing at all.

'You might be interested in this,' he said. 'I spent a great deal of last week studying the by-laws of Carlisle Products.'

'Why bother? Now that you own it you can do as you like.'

'The rules still apply, unless the stockholders approve a change.'

'Which means, since you're the majority stockholder, you can arrange however you please,' snapped Brooke.

'As a matter of fact, I rather like the by-laws the way they are,' Ty mused. 'We need to have a stockholders' meeting, by the way. Now that the fuss of the wedding is over, we can get down to business. Shall we say the first tee at the club, this afternoon at four?'

'A golf course is no place to have a business meeting.'

'On the contrary, my dear. More business is done there than in boardrooms. Frankly, I think it was an inspired choice. If you don't like the agenda, you can take your frustration out on the golf ball, instead of me.'

She shrugged. 'You have to give me appropriate notice, you know. Registered mail, thirty days in advance—that's how Dad always did it.'

'Ah,' he said. 'That's what I love about the by-laws. Elliot may have always done it that way, but he didn't have to. Written notice is all that's required.' He scribbled a few words on a paper napkin and tossed it across the table to her. 'And here's yours.'

She twisted the paper in her hand. 'What happens if I don't show up?'

Ty shrugged. 'Since you and I control the whole company, if you don't come, no business can be taken up.'

'Because with only one stockholder present, it's an illegal meeting,' she said thoughtfully, and smiled. She might yet be able to deal with Tyler! 'You can't force me to come.'

'No. But then I'd just have to keep calling meetings.' He raised his eyes to hers over the rim of his cup. 'If you don't show up at the club this afternoon, the next official meeting might be in your bed tonight.'

It silenced her. She should have expected that he'd have something like that up his sleeve, she thought. That was why he had waited till they were married, and said nothing about Carlisle Products all last week!

'I've suddenly decided that I'm looking forward to nine holes of golf,' she said tartly.

'Eighteen,' Ty corrected. 'We have a lot to talk about. Besides, you'll need some relaxation if you insist on unpacking all those boxes yourself.'

Emily, wearing shorts and a T-shirt, poked her head in the door. 'Darn,' she said. 'We were going to bring you breakfast in bed, but we overslept.'

Brooke stilled a little shiver. That would have been the last straw, she thought. 'Ty made pancakes,' she said.

Emily gave him an approving nod. 'That's the way to Tara's heart, all right,' she said. 'If it's gooey and sweet, she likes it.'

'Pancakes?' Tara repeated hopefully.

Ty pushed his chair back. 'Not only are these my super extraordinary pancakes,' he said, 'but if you young ladies will have a chair, I'll go make some more.'

Emily sighed elaborately. 'This,' she told Brooke, 'is heaven!'

'I wouldn't count on it as an everyday thing,' Brooke told her, and refilled her coffee-cup.

'How was the casserole last night?' asked Emily.

'It was—it was a great idea, Emily. Thanks so much.' Brooke was suddenly very intent on stirring her coffee.

'Did it taste all right? I tried a couple of different ingredients in it.'

'It was wonderful.'

Emily choked, just a little, and Brooke glanced at her sharply. Emily was trying to fight down the giggles. 'Oh, Brooke,' she gasped, 'if you could only see yourself! You never could lie worth a darn!'

'Why, Emily——'

'I'm sorry I couldn't keep a straight face. I was going to pretend I didn't know! Really, I was——' She went off into whoops of laughter again. 'Honestly, Brooke, I'm shocked at you!'

Obviously, no one had fooled Emily. I should have known better than to try, Brooke thought. 'All right,' she said. 'But how did you know?

'Easy as pie. I came down about midnight to clean up

the mess. I put the casserole away and went back to bed. I forgot about the fruit cups—but in any case, you wouldn't have gotten your little cover up past me.'

'Why not?'

'Because we both forgot the champagne.' She gestured at the silver ice bucket on the sideboard. 'The label has probable soaked clear off the bottle by now.'

'Speaking of the champagne,' Brooke began, 'where did you . . . ?'

'I wonder what my wine expert will say about it being chilled and then returned to room temperature. I've heard that it gives beer a funny taste, but I don't know much about champagne.' Emily grinned across the table at her sister. 'Gee, Brooke. And you were so coy about being alone with him at all!'

Brooke thought fleetingly about breaking her plate over Emily's head. Then she realised it would set a very bad example to Tara, who was watching with a great deal of interest as well as confusion in her eyes.

Without a word, Brooke rose from the table, carried her plate back to the kitchen, put it in the dishwasher, and said, almost under her breath, to Ty, 'Emily's in a playful mood, so perhaps I should warn you that I found my bed short-sheeted last night. I'm sure she'd have expected you to have discovered it for yourself, of course.'

'I thought she seemed a bit more angelic than usual yesterday.'

'She's making up for it.' Brooke started on the pile of boxes. 'And to think,' she said, half to herself, 'that I got myself into this mess for her!'

On the first hole, Tyler put his tee shot squarely in the middle of the fairway less than twenty yards from the green. Brooke sighed and walked the few yards to the women's tee.

'This is embarrassing,' she complained. 'I haven't even cleaned my clubs this year, let alone played.'

'Would you care to make any bets on the match?' Ty asked.

'Certainly.' She teed up her ball and promptly sliced it into the rough. 'I'll bet you'll win.'

'No confidence,' he said. 'But if you don't want to play serious golf, I'll call the stockholders' meeting to order. Do we need roll call?'

'Why are you acting as though you've been named chairman of the board?'

'Don't be petty, Brooke. Somebody has to do it, and I'm the majority stockholder.'

'I'd like a vote on that question.'

'Very well. For the position of chairman of the board, I nominate myself. Any further nominations?'

'How about George Washington? We could trust him with the funds.' She didn't even bother to think about her shot, and it arched high over the course and landed prettily on the green. Her chin dropped. 'I've never done that before in my life,' she said.

'Well, don't look blue about it. I vote my fifty-five percent for me. We'll make George honorary treasurer. And furthermore, I'll appoint you as temporary secretary, until we hire a real one.'

'Thanks. Where do I keep notes?'

'The back of the scorecard will do.'

She licked the tip of her pencil, and scribbled on the card. 'Myself was nominated, and Me was elected, as chairman of the board,' she said. 'What's next, O Worthy Leader?'

'Hiring a chief executive officer. I know somebody who'd be great for the job. I just happen to have his résumé right here.'

'Ty——'

'Shhh!' He studied his shot carefully, then chipped on to the green. 'Both of us are on in two—this could be a record day for the club. Now, what were you asking?'

'Why are we even bothering? You have the power. Just do what you want to do.'

'We are bothering, as you put it, because the by-laws say the chairman has to have the approval of the board. These things have to be decided at meetings.'

'Then let's change the by-laws.'

'My fifty-five percent says no.'

'Why?'

'Because the next chairman might not be as reliable a guy as I am.'

'That,' Brooke said tartly, 'is entirely a matter of opinion.'

Tyler two-putted. Brooke, who was further away, sank her ball first try, to her utter astonishment, and won the hole.

They argued their way around the entire course. Brooke's game fluctuated wildly. When she thought about golf, she did very badly, but whenever she was irritably thinking about an answer for Ty, her ball seemed to have a mind of its own.

'We may be on to something here,' mused Ty as they started the last nine. 'And it might be an even better money-maker than typewriter ribbons. Have you ever considered the pro tour?'

'No good,' she said. 'They don't allow hecklers, and without you I'd be lost.'

'I'm glad to find you need me for something.'

It stung just a little, and she was quiet for almost the next hole. Then she said, 'Seriously, Ty, what are you going to do?'

'I'm going back to the pro shop to sign us up for every tournament all summer,' he said. 'We can bet on ourselves and clean up.'

'I meant about Carlisle Products.'

'Oh, that. I don't know—make a few typewriter ribbons, I suppose.' He didn't sound interested.

'You do intend for it to make a profit, don't you?'

'It will be a mighty expensive hobby if it doesn't.'

She made a fatalistic gesture with her putter. 'What I don't understand is how you think you can make it work. Daddy went broke doing exactly that——'

'Your father,' said Ty, hefting his bag for the short walk to the next hole, 'was a charming man. But a businessman he wasn't. I told him exactly what was wrong with his company before I left. But he didn't see it, so he didn't listen.'

'I suppose you intend to make the new kind of ribbons
—your improved kind.'

'In designer colours, I think,' he said. 'Do you think
people would buy a passionate purple ribbon? Or perhaps
if we called it shrinking violet!'

'But the machinery is all outdated, Ty. It'll cost a
fortune to replace it, and if the plant doesn't turn a
profit——'

'It's my money that I'm risking. Or did you have other
plans for spending it?'

Brooke's face froze, and she made the single best shot
of the entire round. 'I don't give a damn about your
money,' she said fiercely, 'or lack of it! So long as Emily
gets through school——'

'Then you must be the only woman in the world for
whom money is not a concern.'

'Well, I wouldn't have expected you to be throwing it
away like water.'

'I think I'm being very careful with it,' Ty said. 'For
instance, take the matter of the Country Club. Your
membership was about to expire, and I couldn't have let
that happen. You've been entirely too much entertainment
for me to give up. So, instead of paying both your dues
and mine, I married you. It makes perfect sense to me.'

'Such logic! Whatever happened to old-fashioned
romance?'

'I don't know,' Ty said, bright-eyed. 'Shall we try to
find some?'

For a moment, Brooke's body felt paralysed. Yes, she
had found herself thinking, I wish I hadn't turned you
away last night . . . Don't be an idiot! she scolded
herself. As if sleeping with him would have solved anything
at all.

She posted her best score ever for the eighteen holes.
By the time they had settled themselves in the lounge, she
was exhausted. 'I haven't walked that whole course in
years,' she said.

'Tired?'

'Too tired to fight with you any more, that's sure. So
tell me, what are you really going to do with the plant?'

'You'll be happy to know that I haven't been resting on my laurels the last few years. I have all kinds of new ideas. We'll be rolling out a newer and even more improved ribbon by the end of the month.'

'You're crazy, Ty!'

'I'm assuming, of course, that some of the former employees want to come back to work. Training new ones would slow me down by a couple of weeks.'

She shook her head. 'You can't even get new machinery here by then.'

'No, I couldn't. What makes you so certain I need any?'

She simply blinked at him.

'You're making the same mistake as your father did, Brooke. It's an inability to think creatively. I didn't design a new ribbon and then figure out how to produce it. When I was still at Carlisle Products, I looked at our declining share of the market, and figured out what we could produce with the machinery we already had. My product was designed with that assembly line in mind.'

'So that's why you wanted it!'

'That's why. I licensed the idea for production, of course, but I never told anybody else the whole secret. Now I can make my own version faster and cheaper then the other manufacturers.'

'You're not playing fair!'

'That, my dear, is how the wonderful world of business operates. All I have to do is go in there by myself with a few wrenches, and no one will ever know quite what I did to those machines. It's a simple thing, really. Then we wait for the raw materials to arrive, and the Carlisle Pride typewriter ribbon will be on the market.'

'It was never called that before,' said Brooke.

'Considering the circumstances, it seemed a fitting name.'

She was hardly listening. 'And you didn't tell Dad how easy it would be?' She was almost angry; Elliot had been frantic, in those last few months, to save his precious business. And Ty could have prevented all that worry!

'Not the details. But of course I told him. He wasn't interested at the time. He didn't see the decline in sales coming as clearly as I did.' He leaned back in his chair and said, as if he was reading her mind, 'No, Brooke, the Carlisle Products failure wasn't my fault. The new process was offered to him, but he was too short-sighted to see the possibilities.'

Or had Elliot been too blinded by his jealousy of this younger man to listen? Brooke wondered again just how much her father had known about Alison and Ty. He must at least have suspected. Elliot hadn't been a fool.

In any case, she thought with a sigh, it was too late for Elliot. But his daughters would benefit. If Tyler was right, the company could eventually be worth far more than ever before.

She looked curiously across the table at him. So there was a chivalrous streak in Tyler Marshall, after all, she thought. Otherwise, he would have bought every share he could, and held all the profits for himself.

And what about Alison? Brooke found herself wondering. What had been her price for the key shares that allowed Tyler to have control? Had she merely given him the voting rights? Or had they struck some bargain?

And why did she even care? Brooke asked herself. Alison was gone; she was no longer part of Brooke's problem.

Or was she? 'Ty—what about Alison?'

He looked up, instantly wary. 'What has Alison to do with it?'

'Why did she sell you that stock? Or did she?'

He looked at her for a long moment. Then he said, slowly and deliberately, 'What happened before our wedding is none of your concern, Brooke.'

She sipped her tea and looked up at him with big green eyes.

Perhaps he was right about that, she thought. Alison was history now. But Ty—Tyler himself was another matter.

She stole a look at him, covertly studying the silvery hair, the strong brown hand that held the iced tea glass. This man she had married, she thought, was a puzzle—a puzzle that it might take a lifetime to understand. She tensed in dread of a lifetime spent with him. And then she realised that it hadn't been dread at all that had sent a tingle of excitement through her.

It had been anticipation.

CHAPTER TEN

THE peonies were in full bloom. Their heavy scent lay over the lawn, still wet with dew under the low sun, as Brooke strolled down across the grass on her early-morning survey. The tree-removal people had finished their work yesterday, leaving only a scar in the earth where the dead oak had stood behind the house. She looked at it for a while, regretting the loss of the big tree that had held her childhood swing. There had been no way to avoid it, of course. The dead wood had to be removed, or a storm would eventually have brought it down against the house. But she still hated to see it gone.

She cut a single large, shaggy flower from the peony bush and slipped the stem through the belt loop on her shorts. It was a white one; when she went back inside she would put it in a vase with food colouring in the water, and watch the flower turn a delicate pastel as the day went on. The bush was loaded with blossoms, and she longed to gather an armful, but she resisted the urge. Peonies were pretty, but their perfume was too strong to have many of them inside.

The lilac was nearly over, she saw, the last delicate-smelling flowers hanging limply on the tree. Summer was fast becoming a reality. Had it actually been less than a week since her wedding? It seemed to Brooke more like a year.

Life at Oakley had already fallen into a new routine. She had wondered idly whether Ty could ever be truly comfortable there, surrounded as he was by females. Not that the question had bothered her, of course; since Ty had chosen to force his way into Oakley, he didn't deserve to be entirely at ease. But he had seemed to have no trouble in adjusting. Of course, she reminded herself, most of the females in the house were delighted to have him there!

Emily, of course, thought he was wonderful. She and Ty had spent endless hours dissecting Cedar College's list of classes, deciding what she should sign up for next week when she went to the orientation session. When they weren't doing that, they were playing chess. More than once Brooke had walked into the silent living-room, thinking no one was there, and found the two of them poring over the board in total concentration. They took their chess seriously and the unwary observer who tried to start a conversation was apt to find himself part of a combat zone.

Tara had hung back, uncharacteristically quiet, for several days, as if reserving judgement. But even she had yielded to Ty's charm by the end of the week, and now the two of them were firm friends. Whenever Tara wasn't at school, it seemed, she was following Ty around, helping him clean out the garage, digging in the garden, going down to the plant with him. Brooke knew it was healthy for the child to have a man around, but she couldn't help feeling a little left out sometimes, when Tara seemed to prefer Ty to herself.

Yes, she thought, Ty had made himself at home. He had systematically set about winning Tara's heart, and he had been careful not to upset Emily's growing fondness for him. He had even charmed Mrs Wilson.

But he had left Brooke strictly alone.

They talked, of course, but it was never about anything important. He would put an arm around her, or drop a casual kiss on her lips sometimes, if one of the girls was there to see. It was never anything more intimate than that—never anything that she would have been embarrassed by. But when they were alone, there was silence, or stilted small talk. There was seldom even a casual chat about their day. She didn't bother any more to try and keep a conversation going. He didn't seem to care whether they talked; he certainly hadn't volunteered another glimpse of his inner thoughts, as he had that night at the club when he had confided his plans for the plant.

It was a mistake to ask him about Alison, Brooke told herself sadly. He obviously had not wanted to lie to her, but he certainly hadn't wanted to confirm the truth, either. And ever since then, he hadn't talked much about anything. The comfortable Ty she had seen that day had retreated into his shell again.

Truthfully, she saw now, perhaps the subject of Alison *was* none of her business. No matter how he had persuaded Alison to give up that stock, it had been done, and it could make no difference to Brooke herself. In the end, she might even be glad of it, she thought, if Carlisle Products became a valuable part of the community again.

Then she pulled herself up short. Glad? she asked herself. Why had she said that? How could she even dream of being glad that she was married to this man who thought nothing of force and blackmail to get his way?

The strain of living like this, she told herself, is unhinging your mind!

In a way, it was a relief to have the girls around. Tara and Emily never had any trouble in keeping a conversation going; there was always something they wanted to talk to Ty about. It made Brooke almost jealous at first, until she realised that both girls were basking in the newness of the situation, happy to have the big brother they had always wanted.

And Brooke could get through the days all right. She could almost pretend that he was no more than a big brother to her, too. The worst times for her were mornings and evenings, when she and Ty were alone in their bedroom. So far, he had been a perfect gentlemen there, with never any hint of a repetition of that first night of their marriage. Every night, he retreated silently to the couch in the sitting-room. He didn't seem to mind at all. In fact, she thought, he sometimes seemed just a little relieved that he didn't have to share her bed.

How could she have been such a fool? she asked herself a hundred times a day. It hadn't been very flattering of Ty to straighten her out so cruelly, but it had been effective. He had made it very plain, by so callously refusing to gratify the desire he had aroused, that the physical attraction he felt for her—while no doubt real—was no more than he would feel for any reasonably attractive woman.

By doing so, she thought sadly, he had awakened a curiosity in her that refused to go away. Whenever he came near her, her body remembered the gentle touch that had aroused such astounding force within her. She found herself avoiding him, trying to prevent an embarrassing repetition. Not that she was afraid of what he would do, precisely, but she was terrified of herself.

It frightened her to think about how easily her defences had broken down in Ty's arms. She had never thought of herself as a passionate woman, exactly. She had always enjoyed being kissed, and she had been confident that when the time came she would be pleased with the physical side of marriage. Ty had never pressed her, and she had been content to wait until they were married. She had assumed that marriage would not, after all, be so very different.

Instead she had discovered on her wedding night, in the arms of a new and confident Ty, that she possessed a very real hunger deep within her that threatened, when released, to consume all common sense. She had felt, for the first time in her life, an overwhelming desire to explore the outer reaches of passion. If Ty hadn't left her that night, she would have begged him to make love to her.

The knowledge had come as a tremendous shock to Brooke. How was it possible, she wondered, that she could detest what Ty had done to her, and yet long for him with every cell of her body?

And what about Ty? she wondered. Just how did he feel about her? She couldn't guess whether he was waiting for a renewed opportunity, or if her behaviour had driven all desire from him. But it looked as if there would be no repetition.

In the first couple of days after the wedding, Ty had come into the bedroom unexpectedly once or twice, and she had reached hastily for a robe. But he had merely looked at her impassively, with one dark eyebrow raised as if to question why she felt that her modesty needed protecting. Now she didn't bother any more. This very morning, he had come in from the sitting-room just as she was getting her clothes, and he had looked furious, and then retreated to the sitting-room as if the sight of her in her underwear was more than he could stand.

She wished it was possible for one of them to move down to the guest-room. At least then perhaps they wouldn't be in each other's way all the time. But as long as the girls were there, they would be confined in the master suite.

I don't know how long I can stand it, she thought. Living this way, with him continually next to me——

'What's the matter, Brooke?' a voice called. 'You look as if you intend to walk clear to the coast this morning!'

Brooke looked up, and was surprised to find herself in front of the Remington Arms apartments. She hadn't even been aware that she had left Oakley behind.

Jane leaned on the fence. 'You had your head down and you were pounding along the sidewalk as if you were running away,' she added.

'I'm working off my frustrations,' Brooke explained.

Jane laughed. 'If it were me, I'd just tell Ty I was frustrated,' she advised. 'I'll bet he knows a few ways to help you get over it! He's the best thing that ever happened to the Friends' group, by the way. Twelve women joined last week. Of course, that was before they knew he was getting married, but some of them will stay anyway.'

'That's something,' said Brooke drily.

'Umm. I can't think why I never thought of that gimmick before—an attractive man as bait, so to speak.'

If I were an ordinary wife, Brooke thought, I'd be more than a little jealous about the idea of a dozen eligible women who want to meet my husband. Instead, I'm just a bit amused. If they knew the whole story, they wouldn't be so eager to scrape an acquaintance with him!

'Will you be at work today?' asked Jane.

'No. It's Tara's last day of school this year, so I took the day off to help with her class picnic. Why?'

'I wanted to talk to you. I've been tinkering with ideas

for our next fund-raising project.'

'No more carnivals?'

'I don't know. We cleared more than two thousand dollars. One more event like that and we can afford to buy the carpet for the whole building. But the next carnival is a whole year away, so surely we could do something in the meantime?'

'Are you still thinking about that recipe book?'

Jane laughed. 'I could bundle all your favourites together and call it Brooke's Cookbook.'

'Not if you want to still be my friend when it's all over.' Brooke glanced at her watch. 'I have to get home. See you tomorrow.'

'What's your hurry?' grinned Jane. 'Oh, I know. Ty's ready to go to work, and you can't let him leave without his goodbye kiss—right?'

Friends, Brooke thought irritably as she walked slowly back towards Oakley. What was it about newlyweds that made people want to say cute things all the time?

Mrs Wilson was already at work, fussing mildly about the mess Ty had made of her kitchen as he scrambled eggs that morning. Brooke half-listened, then put the complaint out of her mind. In the first place, it was only a minor mess; in the second place, Ty would have cleaned it up himself if Mrs Wilson hadn't come in before he had the chance, and in the third place, everyone in Oakley Mills knew that Mrs Wilson adored the man and thought that anything he did was just fine. Her clucking about the state of her kitchen was mere exercise for her throat muscles, Brooke was sure. She left Mrs Wilson muttering to herself, poured herself a cup of coffee, and went on into the dining-room.

Ty was reading the newspaper, but he glanced up as she sat down across from him. 'Did you enjoy your walk?' It was cursory, but at least he'd started a conversation.

She nodded. 'It's lovely and cool this morning. Where's Tara?'

'She left for school a few minutes ago. Emily hasn't come down yet.'

She groped for something else to say, but he had turned

back to the newspaper. She stirred her coffee and watched him, covertly, wondering what he was thinking. Did he regret this farce of a marriage as much as she did? He didn't appear to be having second thoughts, but sometimes she thought she saw an unhappy haze in his eyes. Or was it just her imagination?

Why had he done it, anyway? What had he gained from this whole thing? Oakley, of course. She wondered if it still seemed like such a good deal to him. She'd been looking at the bills before she'd put them on his desk, and she was glad it wasn't she who had to pay them. The cost of removing the dead oak alone would have ruined her budget for a couple of months.

But Oakley couldn't be the whole answer, she thought. Ty was practical, above all other things, and what he had done was hardly a practical solution if all he wanted was a place to live!

'They finished with the tree yesterday,' she said. 'I thought I'd stop at the landscape gardeners' today and ask what season would be best for planting a replacement. If you don't mind, that is.'

'Why would I mind?' He turned a page, and she thought she'd lost his attention again. Then he folded the newspaper and laid it aside. 'Unless you'd rather build the greenhouse there instead.'

There was astonishment in her eyes. 'How did you know about the greenhouse?'

'I found the blueprints for Oakley yesterday. They were in the safe down at the plant.'

'I wondered where they'd gone.'

'It wasn't the best location for them, certainly. Anyway, the blueprints show a greenhouse.'

'There was one, once,' Brooke mused. 'It formed the third wing, straight back from the solarium. Mother told me about it.'

'I always did think this house was a funny shape.'

'It certainly is now, but it was much more symmetrical with the greenhouse attached.'

'What happened to it?' asked Ty.

'When she was a child, one of the trees came down in

a storm and crashed the glass roof in, and Grandfather pulled it all down and extended the lawn.'

'You sound sad,' he observed.

She half-smiled. 'I am, I suppose. It's one of those things that would be nice to have, but it's horribly impractical, Ty. In those days there were servants all over this house. It would take a full-time gardener for the greenhouse alone.'

'Not if you don't try to fill it with plants.'

Brooke laughed. 'In that case, what's the point of having it?'

'It looked to me as if the design might be adaptable for a poolhouse.'

'A swimming-pool?' Brooke's eyes lit up. 'Would it be practical?'

'I don't know. I decided I'd better ask what you thought of the idea before I checked with an architect.'

'I'd love it. But don't for heaven's sake tell Tara what you're thinking about, or you won't have a moment of peace until it's finished!'

'I'll mind the warning.' Ty glanced at his watch. 'I'm supposed to interview job applicants today. And you, Mrs Marshall, have made me late to work.'

It was the first time he had called her that, and also the first time that the title—no matter who used it—hadn't brought a feeling of dread to her. 'I'll have a word with your boss,' Brooke murmured.

'It isn't the boss I'm worried about,' he said. 'But my new secretary is a tartar.' He bent over her chair, one hand resting lightly on her shoulder. 'What are you doing for lunch?'

'Chaperoning a hot-dog roast at the park.'

'In that case, I won't join you.'

'I'll tell Tara you wouldn't come,' she threatened lightly, and looked up into his eyes just as he bent his head to give her his habitual kiss.

He said, just a little unsteadily, 'That's the first time you've smiled at me all week.'

She stopped breathing altogether as she looked up at him. His eyes were almost charcoal grey as he looked down at her for a long moment. She couldn't move, couldn't speak, couldn't avoid his touch. To be perfectly truthful, she didn't want to.

His mouth was gentle. He didn't put so much as a finger on her, and yet she felt as securely bound to her chair as if she had been tied there with ropes. It was a long, warm kiss that made her feel just a little dizzy. It triggered that deep longing again, and she cast caution to the wind. She put a hand up to stroke his hair, and he caught it and held her palm against his cheek. The warmth of him, and the pulse that beat under her fingers, only increased the tension inside her.

His tongue teased, and she relaxed with a sigh and let him kiss her again, longer and deeper. Perhaps he wasn't as uninterested as he had appeared in the last few days, she thought. He had said once that making love to her would be a fringe benefit for him.

And what would be so awful about it, she asked herself, if they were to satisfy their physical desires together? He was her husband, after all, and there was little chance that the situation would change. Their bargain had been made to their mutual satisfaction; neither of them intended to back out, so for the next few years, they would be together. Why shouldn't they try to make something positive of their marriage, even if love was beyond their grasp?

She felt a momentary pang of regret for the kind of love she would have liked to share with her husband, the romantic head-over-heels worship of a knight in shining armour. Ty was no knight but at least he had a sense of humour. And they had things in common—Oakley, for one. It was funny, she thought, that her goals in life ran so closely parallel to Ty's, while Dave Sheridan—who she would have expected to appreciate the history and the sentiment involved—hadn't cared in the least about Oakley. To him it had been merely a house.

Ty murmured, reluctantly, 'Brooke, an entire army couldn't remove me from this house right now, except for one thing.'

'What?' she asked huskily.

'My secretary doesn't have a key to the plant yet, and
she's waiting for me in the parking lot right now. And
there are probably a hundred hopeful job seekers waiting
with her.' He kissed Brooke again, hard and fast, and
straightened up. 'And I'm already half an hour late,' he
added.

Brooke blinked a couple of times, and sighed, and
realised that he was looking down at her with a warmth
in his eyes that she had never seen there before. The look
told her that this discussion wasn't finished, and she felt
herself colour a little under that steady gaze. She had
made a sort of promise, there in his arms, and she
wondered with a touch of panic if she had gone completely
crazy.

She was still thinking about it a couple of hours later, as
she started for the park where Tara and her classmates
were gathered for their last-day-of-school celebration. It
was a perfect day for a picnic, and she walked slowly
along the tree-lined streets, enjoying the sunshine and the
songs of the birds. This little town was the best of all
possible worlds, she thought. She had spent her college
years in a city, and coming home to Oakley had been the
best part of it all.

A horn sounded lightly, and then a car drew up beside
the pavement. 'Want a ride?' asked Dave.

Brooke hesitated. She hadn't talked to him since the
day of her wedding; she had seen him only a couple of
times. Once she had bumped into him in town and once
she had spotted him across the lounge at the club. Both
times he had looked irritable and a little sullen, and he
had had nothing to say. She couldn't make up her mind
if she should accept the hand of friendship, or if she
should just turn and run. 'Sure,' she said finally, and got
in. 'I'm only going to the park.'

He put the car into gear. His jaw was set, and Brooke
felt some misgivings about riding with him when the tyres
squealed as the car pulled away from the kerb. 'I don't

understand you,' he said harshly. 'Brooke, how could you do it?'

She didn't pretend to misunderstand. 'I don't think my reasons for marrying Ty are any of your concern.'

'You could at least have been honest with me! When you told me it wouldn't work for us, you could have added that you'd found the man of your dreams.' The words had a sarcastic twist. 'Or should I say, the wallet of your dreams?'

'I didn't marry Ty for his money.' It was quiet. She didn't expect him to believe it; everyone in town probably thought the same thing.

'You certainly didn't waste any time, once he'd acquired the means to support you. A girl like you,' he said savagely, 'married to that uneducated, social-climbing——'

'Stop the car, please, Dave. I'd rather walk.'

He pressed a little harder on the accelerator instead. 'All Marshall has to recommend him is money. Without that, he'd have been laughed out of the Country Club. No place in town with any class would have him!'

'You're probably right, Dave,' she said thoughtfully. 'And it would be their loss.'

'Some loss,' he sniffed. 'One arrogant fool who thinks a crummy little invention makes him as good as anybody else——'

Brooke was frozen with fury. That Dave dared to say such things at all was bad enough. That he had said them to her——

'That's enough, Dave. Ty is my husband, and I will not listen to a word said against him!'

Dave sneered just a little. 'Isn't that touching,' he said. 'The loving little wife! He must really be impressed by that one. What an act, Brooke! You should take it on the road!' The car screeched into the park with a spray of gravel.

Brooke slammed the door when she got out. Dave had shown his true colours, and the shock of seeing him as he really was left her reeling. It took a lot of nerve to say those things, she thought. He was cruel, and vicious, and wrong. Dead wrong, about Ty.

But the unpleasant memory of herself saying similar things left a sour taste in her mouth. She had said them to salve her pain, because it had hurt so much to find him with Alison in his arms. Now tears sprang to her eyes, and she muttered, 'He's more of a man than Dave will ever be. Ty was born without advantages, and he had to teach himself all the things that Dave was given.'

Once Ty had been an awkward young man, ingenuous, a trifle gauche. Now he was as much a man of the world as any of them. But he was even more than that, for he hadn't forgotten the struggle he had made to improve himself, and the pain he had suffered—pain that people like Dave would never understand. That was what made Ty special. That was part of what she loved about him, what she had always loved about him——

She stumbled on the gravel and went down hard, scraping her hands as she tried to catch herself. She landed on the uneven ground and sat there for an instant, trying to catch her breath. But it was not the fall that had shaken her, it was the blasphemous idea that had suddenly clattered through her head. *Did she still love Ty Marshall?*

No, she told herself. That simply wasn't possible. All that had died four years ago. She simply couldn't love someone who had treated her as Ty had. She had, she reminded herself, caught him with Alison in his arms . . .

But even that didn't have the power to whip her to anger, as it had only weeks ago. Perhaps, her heart whispered, there had been some explanation of his behaviour.

If there was, the unwelcome thought intruded, he would have explained it. But he had refused.

And what of it? Everyone made mistakes. Ty's mistake had been a colossal one, granted, but perhaps now he was trying to make amends. He had never really mistreated her, she decided, though there had been times when she had thought differently. He could have forced her to share her bed with him, but he hadn't. He was making it possible for her to keep Oakley and restore it to a showplace. He was providing a first-class education for Emily. He had been unfailingly kind to Tara—to all of them. And he had refused to be paid back with the only thing of value they owned, the Carlisle Products stock. Instead, he was setting out to make it worth a fortune again, so they would all benefit from his hard work.

His kindness, she thought humbly. That's what's different about Ty. Despite the way I treated him four years ago, he's always been kind to me. Perhaps, if I can reach out to him with that same kindness, we might build something between us yet. Stranger things have happened, she thought.

I know I don't feel the same about him as I did four years ago, she thought. I was very selfish then—perhaps too self-centred to be really in love at all. I don't think I ever even wondered how he felt about things.

And as for love—was that what she was feeling for him? She only knew that she cared what happened to him, and that she wanted him to be happy. She knew that when he kissed her she didn't care what happened to the rest of the world. She knew that despite the tension, she had been more contented in the last few days than ever before.

If that was love, then she loved him. And if it wasn't, then it was still more than she had felt for Dave, or any of the other men she had dated—or even for Ty himself, four long years ago. It was a foundation to build on.

The knuckle nearest the emerald ring had been scraped by the gravel. She inspected the wound gravely, and then stared into the depths of the blue-green stone. That, too, had been a kindness, she thought. She hadn't wanted it, but he had known that the lack of a ring would have caused comment, and he had not wanted her to suffer that. He could have humiliated her in a hundred public ways, but he had not.

She looked at the stone, sparkling in the sunlight, and smiled to herself. He had forgotten the world this morning, too, when he kissed her—for a few minutes at least.

'Tonight when he comes home,' she said softly to herself, 'I'll know . . .'

Tara came up from the playground. 'I have a question,' she announced. 'Why are you sitting in the dust, Brooke?'

Brooke smiled. 'I'm getting ready for the picnic,' she said. 'You can't really enjoy a picnic until your clothes are dirty.'

Tara obviously thought she'd flipped. That's all right, Brooke decided. I'm not so sure I haven't!

They walked slowly back to Oakley from the park in the late afternoon, after the picnic was over. Tara was exhausted from the hours of active games. Brooke was worn out too, but it was a happy kind of tired. She was in no hurry to get home; Ty wouldn't be there for an hour yet. She could think no further than that; she only knew that something wonderful was going to happen soon, and that everything would be different.

As they came up the drive at Oakley, she saw a red two-seater sports car parked at an angle by the back door, nearly blocking the drive. 'Thoughtful place to leave a car,' she muttered sarcastically. She'd have a few things to say to Emily about the driving skills of her friends.

But she didn't get the chance. Emily had seen them coming, and she arrived on the patio at the same instant that Brooke and Tara did. She looked grim.

Brooke swallowed the lecture, and asked, 'Whose car?'

'Whose do you think?'

Brooke looked more closely at the number plates. 'Alison?' she whispered.

'That's right,' Emily said bitterly. 'The Duchess has come home.'

CHAPTER ELEVEN

THE Duchess. Emily had dubbed their stepmother that within weeks after she had moved into Oakley. All the sisters had picked it up, but it was Emily who could always give the title an ironic twist that turned it into a weapon.

Alison, the self-centred little beauty who had married Elliot Carlisle for his money and made their lives miserable, had returned. She had anticipated the crash of Carlisle Products—had Tyler warned her of it? Brooke wondered—and she had left Oakley before the worst had come, taking everything she could get her painted claws into as a settlement. She hadn't filed for divorce, though. That decision, Brooke thought, had been well thought out too. Alison always left her options open. If Elliot had managed the miracle of pulling the company through the hard times, then Alison would have reappeared and charmed her way back into his heart. It wouldn't have been difficult: he had adored her, and had refused to admit to her faults.

And now Alison had come back to Oakley. What had brought her here? It couldn't be coincidental, almost a year after she had left, that she would choose this particular week to turn up. She hadn't even come to Elliot's funeral, so why should she come back now? Fury was building inside Brooke like the steam inside a pressure cooker.

Emily had seen the rage in her face. 'Brooke?' she said, with a tinge of fear in her voice.

'Where is she, Emily?'

'In the living-room. She must still have a key, Brooke. She was in the house before I even saw her. I'm sorry, darling. I feel as if I've failed you.'

'It wasn't your fault. Tara—go and play in your room, please.' Brooks didn't need to repeat the suggestion. Tara had disliked the Duchess quite as much as Emily had, and had avoided her whenever possible.

Alison was curled up in a wing chair. She was petite and dainty, her black hair cut short now and carefully arranged to look casual. She was wearing a white skirt, a lacy red blouse and extraordinarily high-heeled shoes. Brooke knew from past experience that even in those shoes Alison would reach scarcely to her chin. Beside this tiny, dark-haired doll, she had always felt about as graceful as a pregnant elephant.

'Goodness,' Alison said in the sultry voice that Brooke remembered so well. 'I hope I haven't upset you by arriving unannounced, Brooke dear. You look rather hot and irritable. What have you been doing out in the sun? Making mud pies?'

Brooke ignored the sugary sarcasm. 'It does come as a surprise to see you, Alison. I seem to recall you saying, when you left, that you'd never spend another day buried alive in Oakley Mills.'

'How charming of you to be concerned about my state of mind. Of course, things do change, and my animosity towards Oakley Mills has relaxed a bit. I'm sure you understand.' Alison patted the chair beside her. 'Won't you sit down, dear, so we can have a heart-to-heart chat? I do wish I could offer you tea. I asked Emily for a tray nearly an hour ago, but I'm afraid the girl had no better manners now than she did when I left.'

'Emily is not your personal maid,' Brooke said stiffly. 'If you want tea, you'll have to make it yourself.'

Alison shook her head sadly. 'I spoke to Elliot time after time about the bad manners you girls displayed. But he had a blind spot where his daughters were concerned.'

And when it came to you, Brooke thought bitterly, he didn't just have a blind spot—it was total darkness! She sat down. 'Exactly what did bring you back to Oakley, Alison?'

'I came to congratulate the newlyweds, of course.'

'So you know about Ty and me.' Then Brooke regretted

saying it. Alison still had friends in Oakley Mills; one of them might have called her. Or, of course, Ty himself could have told her. And even if he had, it certainly didn't mean that there was anything suspicious about it.

Alison giggled. 'How funny that you would put it just that way, Brooke!'

'I'm afraid I don't see the joke.'

'I was thinking the same thing, you see—wondering if you knew about Ty and me.' The Duchess smiled. 'Of course I knew about your wedding, foolish girl. I knew the plans long before you did. Ty and I have no secrets from each other.'

'And you—approved?' Brooke tried to keep her voice level.

Alison fluttered a hand. 'Of course I approved,' she said. 'Did you expect me to be shocked because Ty was making an advantageous marriage?'

No, Brooke thought. I discovered long ago that you had no decency. But Ty—not Ty, she thought. Her chest was hurting, as if someone had squeezed a steel band around her when she wasn't looking, and was now tightening it, millimetre by millimetre. No wonder Ty hadn't wanted to talk about Alison that night at the club, she mused. Why should it surprise her to find out now that nothing had changed?

Because I wanted so much for it to be all right, she admitted. I wanted him to love me, and I wanted it so terribly that I was certain it would happen.

And I had some reason for thinking that things were changing, she reminded herself. He kissed me this morning as if he was desperate to be close to me, she thought.

'One thing is certain,' she said drily. 'At least Tyler didn't marry me for my money, since I don't have any.'

'That's true. And so you've persuaded yourself that he must care for you? How foolish of you to be taken in! You haven't the vaguest idea what he's really like, have you, Brooke?' Alison asked softly. 'You think you're so bright, but there was never a trick that Ty couldn't have beaten you at. He'll always be three steps ahead of you.'

She looked directly at Brooke, and now the smile was smug.

Was Alison implying that she and Ty had planned this scheme, together? But why would he have allowed her to come to Oakley and upset his comfortable plans? Brooke tried to keep her voice level, but it shook just a little as she asked, 'Why are you here, Alison?'

'You haven't figured it out yet, have you?' Alison looked around the living-room with a satisfied smile. 'I think I'll do this room in mauve,' she said thoughtfully.

'Over my dead body,' Brooke said tightly.

'That would solve the problem neatly, wouldn't it? Ty would inherit, of course, and everything would be perfectly lovely.'

'And then you could marry him. You're actually jealous, Alison!'

'Me?' Alison's laugh trilled. 'Oh, you silly girl! I never wanted to marry Ty. Marriage is so dreadfully boring.'

'I'm sure that cheating on your vows added a little spice to life.'

'That's true. Having Ty around made being married to Elliot almost bearable. But I don't think I'll ever marry again. Marriage takes all the excitement out of living, and frankly, Ty wouldn't make a very comfortable husband, as I'm sure you've already found out. Yes, I think mauve for this room. I'm going to enjoy this redecoration so much, Brooke.' There was a tinge of pity in Alison's eyes as she looked up at Brooke. 'I will have Oakley eventually, you know. I've always intended to have it.'

Brooke was stunned at the woman's gall. 'Then why are you here now? Don't you have enough sense to realise that I'll never leave this house, if you're to have it?'

'Yes, you will. That Carlisle pride of yours will never stand for living under the same roof with your husband's mistress. And you can't kick me out, you know.'

'Watch me! Brooke said fiercely. 'It's my house——'

'Oh, do you want to be embarrassed in front of the whole town?' Alison sounded surprised. 'You will be, you know. I'll just go check into the hotel. You can't keep him from coming there to see me, any more than you could keep him from coming down the hall to my room.'

It was true, but embarrassment be damned, Brooke thought. I will not be made a fool of in my own house!

'And he'll want to come, Brooke. Ty has always been mine. All I've had to do was reach out and claim him.' There was a steel web of certainty under the soft voice.

Brooke closed her eyes in pain. What black magic was it, she wondered, that allowed a woman like Alison to mesmerise a man like Ty, to make him think her perfect? She had done the same with Elliot. What was there about the woman that men found fascinating?

But if he wants Alison so badly, she thought, why did he bother to marry me?

Because he was impatient, Brooke's thoughts ran on. Alison wanted Oakley. The quickest way for Ty to get it was to marry Brooke. He had told her himself that his goal was Oakley——

For his children, she told herself fiercely. For our children——

But had he actually said that? Or had he meant instead the children that Alison would give him?

It made a horrible kind of sense, she thought. Ty could have had any house, in this town, or in any town. Why would he have insisted on Oakley? Pure and simple revenge, she had thought at first—wanting to take the house from her simply because it would wound her pride. But revenge, she had come to understand, didn't fit with his nature. It had puzzled her, the conflict between his tenderness, his kindness, and his determination to have Oakley.

'I told Emily to put my things in the guest-room,' Alison went on. 'It will have to do for now, I suppose. The one I used to have seems to be occupied.' She stood up, as if to say that the discussion was closed.

'The master suite is mine now, Alison.'

'Of course. That would explain the awful colour scheme. I'll have to paint and put new wallpaper up as soon as you go. I couldn't possibly sleep with that looking at me.' She looked thoughtful. 'Even with Ty there to distract me—as wonderful as he is with distractions—I'm afraid it would give me nightmares!'

Brooke was too angry to answer. She clenched her hands on the arms of her chair to keep from ripping the woman's hair out. If Ty were here right now, she thought, I'd tear him into tiny pieces! How could I have been so innocent? How could I have let myself believe that Alison was buried and forgotten? Certainly not from anything Ty had said. He had steadfastly refused to talk about the woman, and Brooke had believed that it was because Alison no longer meant anything to him. Now she saw that the opposite could be just as true—that Ty had not wished to speak of Alison because she was too important . . .

I believed what I wanted to believe, Brooke thought. I have no one to blame but myself.

'We simply must have a long talk some day soon,' Alison purred. 'And you must tell me your opinion of Ty as a husband. Just think, you might even make me change my mind about marrying him. You and I have so very much in common, after all!'

'Oh, do you think so?' snapped Brooke. 'Though I must admit that since the first time you came here, Alison, I've known how common you are!'

The black eyes flashed with anger. It was the first honest emotion, Brooke thought, that she'd seen Alison express, and it was quickly smothered in a gay laugh. 'Your father was always so proud of your quick tongue,' she said.

Brooke felt a little as if she was drowning. 'You sound almighty certain that you know precisely what Ty intends to do,' she said tightly. 'What if he hasn't told you all of it? What if he double-crosses you, Alison?'

'For what? To stay married to you?' Alison laughed. 'Don't be ridiculous, Brooke. He's a boy at heart, you see, but he isn't that stupid.' She paused in the doorway, posed with one hand elegantly pressed against the stone arch, as if she were facing a movie camera. 'Besides,' she added sweetly, 'this wasn't Ty's plan at all. It was mine.'

The shock rocked Brooke as if an earthquake had

started to rumble under her feet. This whole thing, she thought, had been Alison's idea? Ty had been no more than a messenger boy, carrying out the details?

Ty, she thought, with an ache in her throat. It had all been a sham. The kindness had been no more than a cover-up. Not the smallest scrap of gentleness had been real.

But this morning, she thought. That hadn't been her imagination—the gentleness of his kisses, the fiery passion that had held promise of a different sort of future together——

Alison was watching the war in Brooke's face. 'Ty is very charming, isn't he?' she said softly. 'You always were something of a romantic, Brooke. But don't fool yourself into thinking that Ty means anything special by his attentions to you. It's part of his nature, you know. He simply can't resist the opportunity, no matter where or with whom——' She sent a meaningful glance towards the solarium door.

'And that doesn't bother you?'

Alison shrugged. 'Of course not. Ty is looking forward to having it all—you and me, Oakley, and his new-found position of power in this community.'

'But surely you don't plan to share him?'

The Duchess's eyes summed her up coldly. 'If I must,' she said. 'I can certainly outlast you, if that's what you're thinking. She looked around the room as if she already owned it. 'I can't wait to start doing the house over,' she said again.

The arrogance of the woman stunned Brooke. 'That's enough!' she snapped. 'Oakley is still mine, and I set the rules under this roof. Get out, Alison. Give me your key, and get the hell out of my house!'

Alison smiled, and Brooke felt uneasily as if she had played into the woman's hands, doing exactly what Alison had hoped she would.

'Here it is,' she said sweetly, tossing the key across the living-room to Brooke. 'It will be easy to get another, of cause.'

Brooke picked up the key from the carpet and turned

it over and over in her hand. That was true enough, she thought. Even if she changed the locks, Ty would have a key. All he'd have to do would be to make a copy of it for Alison.

'Emily!' Alison called. Bring my luggage back down, immediately!'

'It's still in your car,' Emily said from the doorway. 'I am not your servant.' But her tone was quiet, and she was looking at Brooke. Freckles stood out against her pale skin like dots of ink, and her eyes were wide with pain.

How much of it, Brooke wondered, had Emily heard? I should have told her, she thought. I should have warned her, or sent her away . . .

'I will see you around town,' said Alison. 'That's a promise, Brooke. If you don't believe me, just ask your husband.' She swept out of the door.

'It wasn't true,' Emily said. 'Ty could never—he wouldn't——'

Brooke heard the words, but it seemed to her as if Emily were speaking another language. She started towards the stairs, walking carefully, afraid that her throbbing head would fall off if she tripped.

'Please, Emily,' she said painfully. 'Just forget you ever heard it. And make sure she really leaves.' She didn't stop to see whether Emily obeyed; she climbed the stairs gingerly and went straight to her own room.

She was beyond tears. The rage that overwhelmed her was too deep to be expressed in sobs. It was rage not only against Alison and Ty, but against herself for believing him. Worse than that, for wanting to believe him, telling herself that he felt some fondness for her, for allowing herself to hope that some day he might return the love she had discovered for him. That was what hurt the most, she thought. Even knowing that he had lied to her didn't take away the knowledge that over the last four years she had continued to love the man she had thought him to be.

She sat there for more than an hour, waiting for him, before she realised that he wasn't coming home from work. Then, coldly, she called the hotel and asked to be put through to Alison's room.

Tyler himself answered the telephone. For an instant, the pain of hearing his voice was so strong that she couldn't even move. She had told herself that of course he would be there, but she had expected that Alison would make a show of denying it. She was paralysed by the shock that swept over her. Deep inside, she had still been hoping he had been delayed at the plant, that Alison had been lying, that Ty didn't know anything about this awful mess after all, that he would come in at any moment with that warm glow in his eyes that had sent thrills through her this morning . . .

Had it only been this morning? she thought dully. It was astounding how much a life could change in single day.

'Hello?' Ty said again, crisply. He sounded impatient, Brooke thought. No doubt Alison was waiting for him, and he was anxious to get back to her bed. Perhaps he was there right now, and she was snuggled up against his broad chest, impatient for him to finish this call——

Brooke put the phone down with a sharp little click, without saying a word, and sat there by her dressing table methodically chipping the polish from her fingernails, with all her attention focused on the task as if nothing else existed.

There was a tap at her door, and Tara peeped in. 'Emmy said you weren't feeling well,' she said.

'Not very,' Brooke answered honestly. Why, she thought, did I believe Ty for a single moment? Now he has us all in his power. Emily and Tara and me. He'll take Oakley, and we'll be even worse off than we were before. Why, why did I marry him? Emily's plans for college seemed very small and unimportant.

From deep within her came the answer. The money for Emily's education had been an excuse, that was all. She had lied to herself, and refused to face the truth. She had married Ty because she loved him, and because—despite the hurt of four years ago—she had trusted him. Because she had believed in his honesty, and she had known, deep in her heart, that he was the man she wanted—the only man she had ever wanted.

What a lot of sentimental claptrap! She had let herself be taken in by his promises, and now they would all pay for her mistake.

Tara crept into her arms. 'Is the Duchess coming back to stay?'

'No. I promise you that,Tara. You won't have to live with Alison ever again.'

'I'm afraid of her,' Tara confided.

You're not the only one, Brooke wanted to say. She soothed the child and sent her down to have her dinner. The evening crept by, and darkness fell. It was late when Ty came in.

She didn't look up. She knew, though, that he stood in the doorway watching her for several minutes before he came across the room. 'I'm sorry I'm late,' he said.

'Where have you been?' She tried to keep her voice even.

He was silent, as if assessing what story she might accept. There were lines of strain around his eyes, lines that she had never seen there before.

'Don't bother to lie to me,' she said finally. Her nerves were stretched too far to bear any more silence. 'I know you've been with Alison.'

'It was you on the telephone, then.' He put a gentle hand on her shoulder. 'I thought it might be.'

She shuddered away from him. 'Don't touch me,' she ordered. 'Don't you dare lay a finger on me!'

'Brooke, what's the matter with you? I thought—this morning you didn't object at all when I touched you.'

'That was this morning. I've since changed my mind.' She started to file her nails, just to give herself something to do, and to avoid having to look at him. The emery board rasping harshly with every stroke. She noticed, then, that he held a brightly wrapped box, long and flat. 'What's that?' she asked.

He looked down at the box, as if surprised to find it in his hand, and laid it on the corner of her dressing table.

'Just a little something for you,' he said. His mouth twisted fractionally.

'How charming.' Her voice was brittle. 'Can I expect a gift every time you spend an evening with Alison?'

'It wasn't what you think.'

'No,' she agreed tightly. 'It's probably a great deal worse.' Her hands were shaking. 'Did you enjoy making love to her tonight?' She saw him start to shake his head, and added quickly, 'Don't bother to tell me you didn't, Ty. I wouldn't believe you for a moment.'

His words seemed to come from a long way away. 'Then I won't trouble to deny it.'

'Good.' Her voice was hard, taut. 'That's the only way for us now, Ty. Brutal honesty. Because, you see, I'm not going to play your game. I refuse to run away and leave you and Alison with Oakley. I'm staying here, and I'll hold you to your promise.' How? she wondered, in sudden panic. She couldn't force him to honour the pledges he had made!

'Do as you like,' she went on. 'Keep Alison in the hotel, or get her an apartment—whatever you want. But don't bring her into this house, in front of my sisters. Leave them the little respect they still have for you.'

'And you, Brooke?' His voice was quiet, deep.

'If you're asking about my respect for you—my God, how I despise you, Ty! I hate you so much that I think if I had slept with you, I'd kill myself right now in shame!'

For a split second, she thought he might be comtemplating murder, just to save her the trouble. He was fighting for self-control, that much was obvious. He turned on his heel and went to the door.

She picked up the brightly wrapped package and flung it at him. 'Keep your filthy trinkets, Ty Marshall. Carlisles can't be bought.'

The box hit squarely in the middle of his back and bounced on the carpet. He wheeled around with fury in his face, picked it up, and started towards her.

Brooke tried to make herself invisible. She shrank away from him, terrified that she had pushed him over the brink of violence.

'You're an expensive luxury, that's certain,' he said. His voice was hard, and there was no gentleness as his hand clamped on her chin and forced her to look up at him. 'And to think you represent a way of life I thought I wanted,' he said. 'It isn't worth it. Thanks for the lesson, Brooke.'

He dropped the battered package in the waste paper basket and strode to the door.

'Go to hell, Ty!' she called after him.

He paused and started to turn; then, as if exerting every ounce of self-control he possessed, his shoulders straightened and he left the room, shutting the door quietly behind him. In an odd way, it was more final than if he had slammed it.

Brooke's horror eased slowly. She had meant it, she told herself fiercely. She had meant every word of it, and she wasn't sorry she had said it. But she had been so frightened there for a moment. He had looked like death, as if he could have strangled her without a second thought.

What did he expect? she asked herself wearily. That I would agree to it? That I would gladly share him with her, and welcome him in my bed whenever he chose to honour me with his presence? Perhaps even invite Alison to use the guest-room, just to keep everything cosy——

I should have seen it coming, she thought bitterly. Anybody who knew Alison should have expected that this sort of thing would happen. Anybody who knew Alison knew what a schemer she was . . .

Certainly Brooke knew. She had years of experience with Alison's devious ways. And yet she had believed every word that Alison had told her today.

'Come off it,' she told herself wearily. 'He certainly didn't deny it. And it fits together too perfectly with what I already knew, and what happened four years ago——'

Or did it? Nothing that Alison had said explained Ty's unwillingness to take the stock they owned. And Alison had said nothing about Emily's education. Was it possible she didn't know about that part of the agreement? Had Alison been lying? Or had Ty been playing a deeper game of his own, deeper than anyone knew?

'And what difference does it make?' Brooke asked
herself crossly. She flung herself down across the
bedspread, and the first tears seared her delicate skin. He
had not defended himself, and so there was no choice but
to consider him guilty.

'But it doesn't matter,' she whispered into her pillow.
'I still love him.'

He had finally done it, she realised while she lay there.
He had told her more than once that he would break her
pride, and he had finally done it. But it wasn't the threats,
the humiliation, the feeling of powerlessness, the threat of
losing Oakley, that had humbled her. It was the knowledge that no matter what he had done, or why, she still
wanted him. That was why she had so firmly refused to
leave Oakley.

What was it he had said? 'You represent a way of life
I thought I wanted.' It hadn't just been for Alison that
he had married her, Brooke understood. She had forgotten
about that part of it. Her heart suddenly wanted to sing.

'I can fight for him,' she told herself. 'I'm his wife.
Alison can't change that. This morning, he wanted
me—that wasn't my imagination. I can fight——'

She dried her tears and sat up. The bright wrapping of
the package caught her eye, and she pulled the little box
from the waste paper basket and ripped the paper off.
The box opened at a touch, and she stared down at a
solitaire emerald on a fine chain. The centre stone was
surrounded by baguette diamonds pieced into a ruffled
ballerina setting. It was the mate to her engagement ring.

The necklace could not have been a last-minute thought,
she knew. This had been especially made for her. He does
care for me, she thought. He does!

Anticipation began to pound through her. She took the
stairs at a run. 'Ty!' she called at the foot of the staircase.
There was no answer.

The door of the little study was closed. She went to it,
trying to organise the words of apology in her head. I
was hasty, she would say. I didn't want to believe what
Alison told me, but she was so coldly logical about it——

'He isn't there.' Emily was in the living-room. She

turned back to the chessboard to study the position of
the pieces. But her voice was lifeless, and Brooke had the
feeling that Emily didn't see the ivory chessmen at all.

'What do you mean? Where is he?'

Emily shrugged. 'He didn't tell me where he was going.'

'He's gone?' Brooke's voice was a bare whisper.

'Yeah.' Emily looked up, and Brooke was stunned to
see her shock-wide eyes. 'He said to give you this.' She
put a small hard object in Brooke's hand.

Brooke stood frozen, looking down at the brass door
key that winked up from her palm. Emily was right, then.
He was gone. And he had no intention of coming back.

CHAPTER TWELVE

BROOKE sat down on the bottom step, hard.

Emily looked down at her with tear-bright eyes. Her voice was shaky. 'I don't know what you said to him. But he's never coming back, Brooke! You sent him away——'

'Dammit, Emily! For once in your life would you be on my side?'

Emily stared down at her sister for a long moment. Never had Brooke spoken to her so sharply, and for an instant the girl seemed stunned. Then she shook her head firmly. 'Not when I think you're dead wrong, Brooke.'

'You haven't any idea what you're talking about.'

'Perhaps I don't know every detail,' the girl admitted. 'But I know Ty, and I know Alison—and I know which one of them I'd trust. I can't understand why you would believe what the Duchess told you, Brooke. You know what a liar she is!'

'Yes. I know.' And I also know that Ty is no more trustworthy, she thought wearily. Or was it possible that Emily was right? Alison was capable of anything. But would she have dared to come to Oakley, to sit there and talk to Brooke like that if it wasn't all true?

Brooke didn't know. All she understood was that Ty had gone and she felt sick about it. He had, without a doubt, gone back to Alison at the hotel.

I could find out for sure, she thought. All I have to do is call. But what did it matter? It certainly wouldn't change the facts, and having the truth thrust in her face would be more than she could bear.

She pulled herself up from the carpet, and started upstairs. The staircase looked endless, and she was so unbearably tired that she didn't know if she could make it.

She didn't sleep. She lay across her bed, thinking about Emily's blind faith in Tyler. I'm going to have to tell Emily everything, she thought. Perhaps I should never have tried to keep it away from her at all. Emily's an adult now, but I've kept treating her as a child.

'I didn't want to destroy her affection for Ty,' she muttered. 'What a joke!'

She tried to straighten out in her mind what she would tell Emily. She went over and over it in her head. Finally, unable to stand the chorus of voices in her brain any more, she went down the hall to her sister's room.

'Emmy?' she called softly.

She had almost given up when the soft answer came. 'Come in.'

Emily was sitting on the windowseat with her feet up, her arms wrapped around her knees. She was wearing pyjamas, but her bed had not even been turned down. Moonlight pouring in at the window turned her fair hair to silver, and brought an ache to Brooke's heart.

She sat down beside Emily, and told her everything, starting from the day in the solarium four years before. Emily flinched a little, now and then, but she didn't say a word through the whole story. When she had finished, Brooke stared out over the moonlit lawn, and waited while Emily turned it over in her mind.

Finally the girl said, 'I admit it looks suspicious.'

Brooke shrugged her shoulders. 'It certainly does.'

Emily added obstinately, 'But it only appears that way because of what Alison told you. Take that away, and what's left?'

'Quite a lot. Ty married me for two reasons—because I'm a Carlisle, and to get Oakley for Alison.'

'Explain to me how being divorced from you is going to help his social acceptability.'

Brooke bit her lip. 'It wouldn't,' she admitted. 'But he doesn't plan to divorce me.'

'It won't take long for word to get around about Alison, and his new reputation would be shot anyway. He knows that. So why did he marry you? You just told me that he had a plan to get Oakley away from you, anyway. Neither reason holds up when you look at it, Brooke.'

'Emily, stop practising your courtroom skills on me!'

Emily shrugged. 'Very well,' she said. 'I'd like the answer to one more question. Then I'll quit.'

Brooke could see the question coming. Emily would ask, How do you feel about Ty? Brooke braced herself, and wondered what she could say that would be true, and yet not devastatingly honest.

But Emily asked instead, 'Am I still going to Cedar College? Or did that go down the drain tonight too?'

'Oh, Emmy—I'm sorry.' Brooke had forgotten the consequences to Emily; now everything she had tried to achieve with that foolish marriage was gone, and all she was left with was ruined dreams. She wiped tears away. 'I'll talk to Ty in the morning. That's a promise——'

'If it's all the same to you, Brooke, I'd rather you stayed out of it. I'll talk to him myself.' Emily's tone was dry.

'I guess I can't blame you. I have made a muddle of it, haven't I?'

'It's a good thing for you that I'm not already a member of the bar,' Emily agreed. 'I'd sue you for malpractice as my guardian.'

Brooke forced a laugh. It was painful, but it helped a little. 'I'm sure Ty won't be unsympathetic,' she said. 'He may still agree to loan you the money . . . '

'You see?' Emily was triumphant. 'That proves my point! I knew you still trusted him, underneath. If it hadn't been for all that garbage of Alison's——'

'All that garbage, as you put it, fits very neatly with what I already knew.'

'No, it doesn't. I've blown holes in your logic. I can keep doing it till the sun comes up. But you just said the important thing—you still think Ty will make sure I get through school. That's got nothing to do with Alison, or Oakley, or anything but the kind of person Ty is.'

'I hope you're right, Emily. For your sake.'

'For all our sakes,' said Emily. She sounded like the voice of doom. 'This was all my fault, you know.'

'Because you wanted to go to Cedar? Oh, Emily, please don't blame yourself. I chose to get myself into this mess!'

'No,' Emily said softly. 'That's not what I meant at all. It's my fault, because I'm the one who called the plant and told Ty that Alison came here today, and that she went to the hotel.'

Alison herself hadn't told him that she was coming? He had gone there to talk to her, and—what had he said? I didn't give him a chance to tell me, Brooke thought. I assumed that I already knew. I assumed he was guilty because of what Alison told me, and I drove him back into her arms.

If there had been even a fragile hope for them, she had destroyed it with the words she had flung at him in their bedroom tonight. The trust that had been slowly building between them was gone, ripped to shreds by a vicious woman's catty words, and by the razor-sharp accusations that had grown from Brooke's own jealous hurt.

Alison had built tiny bits of information into what looked like a web of conspiracy, a trap into which Brooke had fallen neatly without even checking to see if it might have been false. I played straight into her hands, Brooke thought. I gave him back to her on a silver platter.

And, now that she knew that all she wanted was Ty—no matter how, or on what terms—it was much too late to do anything about it.

Two days went by in silence. Brooke didn't hear from Ty; she hadn't really expected to, though she knew that some day soon they'd have to talk. Surely now he would want to end this marriage? She shied away from the thought, though she knew that the longer it went on, the more painful and public the final break-up would be.

Emily went down to the plant and talked to him, then came back to Oakley and started to pack his clothes. Brooke found her in the master bedroom, clothes stacked all over the bed, and took over the job herself.

'What did he say?' she asked as she carefully laid piles

of folded shirts into the single leather bag he had brought with him.

'No message for you, if that's what you're asking. I'm going to Cedar.'

Brooke bit her lip. She should be glad for Emily, she thought, and happy to have her instincts about Ty confirmed. Instead, sadness and longing tugged at her. She found herself caressing a silk shirt as if it had been his skin, and forced herself to stop. I had everything I wanted in the world, she thought, and I threw it away. I was too stupid to recognise it when I saw it.

The two days that had gone by had helped her to see things more clearly. She knew, now, that she hadn't been imagining her love for him. She missed him horribly. A hundred times a day she wanted to turn to him with a comment or a question. She wanted to share with him the beauty of the sunset, to ask him what she should do about the couch grass in the lawn, to laugh with him about how funny Tara had been at breakfast that morning.

Don't be silly, she told herself. You never shared those things before. When he was here, you never talked about anything important.

Because I held myself aloof from him, she admitted. Because I was afraid to get too close to him, for fear that he would hurt me again. Instead, I hurt myself. If I'd been anything less than cold to him, things would have been different.

If I can only have him back, she thought, I don't care about the rest.

But what if Alison had been right? What if he did want them both?

I can't, she thought. I couldn't stand to share him, to know when he came home that he'd been with her.

In any case, she thought, there was no point in thinking about what she would do. She wouldn't have another chance.

That week, an early heatwave hit. The library was like an oven. Even in the morning, it was hot inside, and as the sun beat down on the roof, the temperature inside grew unbearable.

Brooke gritted her teeth and worked through the heat, and tried not to think of the new building that might have been, if things had gone differently all those years ago.

'You look like a wilted lettuce leaf,' Jane accused Brooke, late one afternoon. 'What's the matter with you lately?'

Brooke had scarcely heard the question. 'It's just so blasted hot! Everybody's temper is on edge.' Tara had been in tears at the breakfast table that morning; when pressed for an explanation, she had announced sullenly that she missed Ty. Emily had rolled her eyes and asked Brooke when in heaven's name she was going to do something about it. Brooke had started to cry, which had horrified both her sisters, and then she had run out of the room. Yes, everybody's temper was on edge.

'At least Emily's leaving for her orientation and tennis camp tomorrow,' Brooke said. 'It will be a little more peaceful around Oakley.'

'I bet you'll be glad. I can't wait to get to the lake,' said Jane. 'We're leaving tomorrow morning. Hey, would Tara like to go along? It's cool up there, and she'll be no trouble to me. It'll give you and Ty a chance to be alone.'

There was no sarcasm in her tone, and Brooke nearly dropped the stack of magazines that she was carrying. Was it possible that Jane didn't know? The whole town should have heard about it by now . . .

'I'll ask her,' she said. 'Tara always did like the lake.' And perhaps by the time the girls both get home, she thought, I will have found some peace within myself, and I'll know what it is that I want to do.

She saw Tara off the next morning, with sleeping bag, insect repellent, and suntan lotion. Emily left that afternoon on the bus, with her tennis racquet, a wardrobe selected to impress the males on the team, and enough excitement to supply the whole town. Brooke went home to an empty Oakley and looked hard at a future that horrified her.

That night, she dreamed that Ty was there beside her. She could taste his kisses, feel the gentle touch of his hands. For the first time in nearly a week she was happy. Then she woke, and found herself alone, and the awful blackness of despair settled around her again.

She paced the floor until morning came, facing the fact that he wasn't going to come back. She also knew that she was miserable, and that she could not begin to feel better until she had at least apologised to him.

That morning, she ventured into the small study for the first time since he had gone, and took the cover off the typewriter. It took the best part of an hour, and a dozen sheets of paper, before she had finished a single neatly typed page. She read it over once more, and put it in an envelope. If she got it to the post office quickly, he would pick it up today when he got the rest of the mail for the plant.

For the rest of the day, her heart seemed to be fluttering about wildly, bouncing from her toes to her throat, as she wondered what would happen. He might tear it up, or not even bother to open it. And even if he read it, he might ignore it entirely. She tried to keep herself from hoping, and she was glad that Jane wasn't there, or Emily with her all-seeing eyes. She forced herself to work on the library's budget, but the figures made little more sense than random numbers would have. Finally, it was closing time. She turned the key with a sense of relief, and went home.

But the tension mounted as the evening wore on. Finally, she could stand it no longer and started off on foot towards the little park. Would he come? What if the envelope hadn't been delivered to him after all? Had she simply made a fool of herself all over again?

She settled herself on her chosen bench, the one closest to the shadowed place where they had always spread their blanket on band concert nights. They had been happy here, she thought. The park held no uncomfortable memories to interfere with what had to be done.

Her hands were clasped so tightly in her lap that the emerald ring cut grooves in her skin. But she didn't feel pain. She was beyond feeling very much at all just now.

Eight o'clock had been the hour she had given him. At

that hour the park would be nearly deserted, yet it was early enough that he could make some excuse to Alison for his absence.

She shifted restlessly on the bench, and her copy of the page she had sent him rustled in her pocket. There was still light enough in the dusky sky to read it, but she didn't have to. She knew it by heart. 'Special meeting of Carlisle Products stockholders' it was headed, followed by an agenda.

Would it touch his curiosity? Or had he finished with her entirely?

The minutes crept by. Eight o'clock came, and passed. By eight-thirty, hope had died, and anger was beginning to take its place. Would he refuse to give her a few minutes, on neutral territory, long enough for her to tell him she was sorry? Couldn't he leave Alison's side for that long, at least?

There was a public telephone in the park. She fumbled in her pocket and found some change. Well, he'd hear it whether he wanted to or not, she decided fiercely. He couldn't avoid her entirely!

The hotel desk clerk seemed astounded. 'Mrs Carlisle? Mrs Alison Carlisle? I have no such name listed.'

Brooke readjusted her grip on the receiver. 'Then would you ring Mr Marshall's room, please. Mr Tyler Marshall.'

There was a momentary silence. 'Mr Marshall checked out about two weeks ago,' he said.

I know that, dummy, Brooke wanted to retort. It was my wedding day. 'Yes, but he's been staying there since.'

'I have no record of Mr Marshall returning.'

She licked dry lips. 'And Mrs Carlisle has left?'

'She stayed with us just one night, ma'am.'

'I see.' Brooke put the telephone down and leaned against the side of the booth, heartsick. Had they moved into an apartment somewhere? Or, for that matter, had they left town altogether? It was odd, now that she stopped to think about it, that no one had mentioned seeing Alison around. Brooke had never considered checking at the Carlisle plant to see if Ty was still coming to work. Emily had taken his luggage down to him the day after their quarrel, but if she had seen him since then, she had said nothing to Brooke.

What a fool you are, she told herself. You still thought, deep down, that you could fight Alison and win, that because you wear his ring you had some sort of advantage over her.

Her head drooped as she started wearily for home, idly playing the game of don't-step-on-a-crack, trying to keep her mind occupied with something for fear that if she didn't, she might just start howling at the moon.

She didn't even notice that there was a car following her until it speeded up, turned abruptly into a drive just ahead of her, and blocked her path. She nearly walked into the side of it before she stopped herself.

It was Ty's car. Her heart started to pound.

The passenger door was pushed open from inside. 'Get in, you little fool,' he said, his voice harsh. 'You deserve to be mugged, wandering around town at this hour of the night!'

'No thanks to you,' she said. 'If you'd been on time——'

'You're lucky I'm here at all. I only picked up the mail a few minutes ago.'

'Oh? Have you been too busy with other things to worry about little things like business?' Then she bit her tongue. This was no way to start what was supposed to be an abject apology.

He didn't answer. She couldn't see his face in the darkness of the car, but she knew from the way he drove that he was furious. He took her back to the park and stopped the car next to the bench she had been sitting on such a short time ago. 'I don't know what the hell you're up to,' he said, 'but here we are.'

'I'm a stockholder. I have every right to arrange a meeting. You said yourself all it took was written notice.'

'All right, I'll play along. I call the meeting to order.' He shut the engine off, and reached into his pocket for a sheet of paper that crackled as he unfolded it. 'The first item on this cute little agenda, under old business, is a statement by Mrs Marshall. Well, Mrs Marshall, just what is it that you wanted so badly to tell me?'

Brooke was trembling, and her throat was tight. Why had she ever imagined that all she needed to do was get him alone and tell him she was sorry? As if that could make everything all right!

She swallowed hard. 'I wanted to tell you that I was wrong. I should have listened to you that night.'

There was a long silence. She couldn't think of anything else to say. Finally, Ty said drily, 'Is that why we went to all this trouble? So you could say that?'

'Ty, please! I really am sorry. I jumped to conclusions, and I don't blame you for being angry.'

'I accept your apology.' It was quiet, cool, with not a shred of emotion about it.

Another silence, and Brooke began to feel angry because he was making no attempt to meet her half-way. 'You have to admit that I had good reason not to believe you,' she said at last. 'You did have an affair with her. With my stepmother, for heaven's sake! So when she told me——'

'No.' He said it through gritted teeth.

'What do you mean, no?'

'I said, no. I did not have an affair with Alison.'

'Ty, I know what I saw.' She stared at him in the darkness. 'You were kissing her in the solarium.' Brooke stopped dead. Just what had she seen? she wondered now. Alison had been in Ty's arms, that was certain. But she had assumed the rest, because of what Alison had said, and what Ty had refused to talk about . . .

'She asked me to come to Oakley that day,' he said. 'She told me that she was concerned for me, that she thought I should know the truth about you——'

'About me?' Brooke said sceptically.

'Yes. She told me that she was afraid I'd be hurt, that everyone knew you weren't serious about me, and that you had even announced that you'd become engaged to me just to prove you could do it. She warned me that you were about to dump me——'

Brooke shook her head. 'What does that have to do with you kissing her?'

'She gave a friendly hug to comfort me and let me

know she was on my side.' Ty's voice was clipped, crisp. 'At least, that's what I thought at that instant. Suddenly she was kissing me, and I didn't know what the hell to do. I couldn't seem to peel the woman away. And then you came in.'

The ring of truth was in his words. Brooke tried to swallow the lump in her throat.

'She planned it, Brooke,' he said. 'She wanted you to see us.'

'Why didn't you tell me?' Her voice was hollow.

He laughed, without humour. 'What could I say? No matter what the truth was, if I'd told you what she said, you'd have denied it. I couldn't tell you what she'd said.'

And Alison had known that very well, Brooke thought.

'So I decided to wait, to be on my guard, and to watch you very carefully. Then I'd know whether Alison was right. If you loved me, you would take my word about it, I thought. But you didn't believe me.'

'I couldn't trust you, Ty, when you wouldn't explain! It was pretty damning, you must admit——'

He interrupted ruthlessly. 'In any case, you didn't give me a chance to explain. You broke our engagement before I had time to even think about telling you what she'd said. It was all the confirmation I needed that Alison had been right after all—that you'd just been playing with me. And when you told me in the garden a few days later that you'd never intended to marry me——'

'Oh, my God.' It was a mere breath. My disastrously quick tongue, Brooke thought. I walked right into Alison's trap. She planned it that way, the she-devil!

'So I went away,' Ty said, very quietly.

'Then why——' She stopped, swallowed hard, and tried again. 'Why did you come back, Ty?'

He stared straight ahead. His hands were clenched on the wheel. 'It hardly matters now, does it? I wish to hell I hadn't.'

It was the death of hope. 'You're right,' she agreed sadly. 'It doesn't matter now.' She opened the door and stepped out on the gravel of the park drive. 'Thank you for letting me apologise.'

He didn't answer, and she took a few uncertain steps away from the car. Then, as if a hammer had hit her in the head, she realised that she couldn't stop there. If it took every shred of honesty in her, she had to finish this. To stop now would be to put her pride above everything else, again.

She retraced her steps. His window was down, and she leaned on the door and said, 'Dammit, Ty, it matters to me! Why did you come here? Why did you marry me at all?'

He didn't look at her. 'Get in, Brooke. I'll drive you home.'

She slid into the car, and he started the engine.

'Did you ever love me?' she asked, so quietly that she didn't think he could hear.

He sighed. 'I suppose I must have. At least I thought I did.'

'But I killed that, didn't I?'

There was no answer. The few minutes that it took to drive to Oakley were silent.

'You aren't going to tell me, are you, Ty?'

'Why don't you just fill in whatever answer you like best?'

'Oakley,' she said. 'And the plant. And the family connections . . . '

'Close enough.'

She took a deep breath, and pushed her pride into a back corner of her mind. 'That was the bargain we made,' she said. 'I plan to keep it, Ty.'

He sighed. 'I release you from all promises.'

There was dead silence in the car as he parked it by the back door. Brooke stared at the headlights reflecting dully back at her from the brick walls. She studied the pattern of light and shadow as if she were trying to memorise it.

'Then—do you want Alison after all?'

He said, harshly, 'God, no. I never wanted Alison. I never even saw her again till after your father's funeral, when I bought her stock. And I would never have seen her after that if she hadn't turned up here.'

'What happened at the hotel that night?' Her voice was

a bare whisper. Would he tell her, or would he once more refuse to explain himself?

'She propositioned me. I told her I wasn't interested, and suggested that she leave town in a hurry. She laughed and shrugged and said it had been worth a try. She was packing when the telephone rang. I thought it must be you, and I wasn't going to let her get another stab at you. So I answered it.'

It was a simple narrative, but Brooke could almost see the scene that must have taken place.

'She's always hated you, Brooke—and apparently she hasn't been exactly fond of me either, after she heard that the stock she sold me for a pittance was the key to the whole operation.'

'She didn't hold you up for money?'

'She tried,' he said grimly. 'But she was almost broke, and I knew it.' He shifted impatiently in the seat.

'We were both afraid, four years ago,' she said. 'You were frightened that I was playing with you, and I was afraid that you were in love with Alison, and that you'd only proposed to me because of who I was. I was too dumb to think about what I was throwing away, too dumb to ask myself if it even mattered why you wanted to marry me. Now, I don't care. I still love you, Ty. I've always loved you. And I want you back, under any circumstances.'

He was silent for what seemed hours. Her courage deserted her. He had talked about her pride, but she was certain of only one thing—that she didn't have enough pride to hold her upright while he ever so kindly told her that he didn't care any more, and that Oakley was no longer enough to hold him.

She pushed the car door open, clumsily. 'I understand, Ty,' she said. 'You don't have to tell me——' Tears blurred her eyes, and she stumbled over Tara's bike on the patio. Finally she reached the back door, and huddled against it, fumbling for her key.

The car engine died, and then suddenly Ty's hand was warm on her bare arm. 'I think we have one more piece of unfinished business on the agenda,' he said. 'You still owe me a kiss from the carnival . . . '

Her heart started to pound, long, shuddering blows
that echoed through her body. She looked up at him in
the dim light, afraid to believe she was hearing correctly.
Then, with a sigh, she brushed her fingertips gently through
his hair, and raised her face to his.

I don't care if he loves me, she thought. I love him
enough for both of us.

It was like no other kiss she had ever experienced. She
stood on her toes and pressed herself against him to stop
the trembling, but that only made her more light-headed.

'It's a good thing,' Ty murmured against her lips, 'that
you weren't handing out kisses like this the day of the
carnival. Jane would have been overrun with new members,
and I would have been chewing the furniture with jealousy!'

'Would you?' she asked, and kissed him again before
he could answer.

Finally he said, 'You pack quite a punch, my love.'

Brooke stopped breathing. It's only a word, she
reminded herself.

He sighed, wearily, and shifted his grip, pulling her so
close to him that she could feel every beat of his heart. 'I
thought it would be safe to come back. Four years—I'd
gotten over you, and I wanted to pay my respects to your
father. But that day at his funeral——'

'You were there?'

'Yes. I saw you come into the church, with Emily and
Tara beside you. I didn't hear another word. You were
so beautiful, and I knew then that I'd never get over you,
that I will love you till I die.'

She smiled up at him mistily. For a moment, she
thought, he had sounded very much like the shy young
man who had put that chip of a diamond on her finger.

'I didn't go to the cemetery. I went to the plant instead.
I knew Elliot was in trouble, but it wasn't until I heard
the talk around town that day that I knew how bad it
was.'

She snuggled her head into his shoulder.

'And I began to think that perhaps my unreachable

goal was back within my grasp, after all.'

'You kept telling me that you didn't love me any more.'

'Did you expect me to admit it—and give you that sort of power over me?'

'No,' she whispered. She could hardly breathe.

'I kept telling myself that love didn't matter any more, and that what I planned to do was all right.'

'But I don't understand. If you wanted to marry me, why did you offer to buy the stock?'

He sighed. 'You have to understand that forcing you into marriage was not my original idea. I hoped you might have mellowed a bit. I thought you might even discover that you'd missed me a little. Instead, you went off like a firecracker any time I came near you. So Plan B came into existence!'

'What would you have done if I'd sold you the stock?'

'I'd have given it back to you as a wedding present. But I have to admit that I didn't try very hard to make you want to sell it. I think I was afraid that if I let go of that hold on you, you'd slip out of my grasp entirely.'

'I regretted not taking your last offer. Even Ben Adams thought I was crazy—he was astonished that you'd offered me so much.'

'Are you certain? He got ninety dollars a share for his.'

'Why, you rat!' Brooke drew a fraction of an inch away, pretending horror.

Ty pulled her back against his broad chest again. 'Look at the positive side. Ben got mere money. You still have your stock, and you also have me.'

'What a dividend!' she said demurely.

'You didn't seem to think so on our wedding night. When you made your grand offer to submit to my animal lust . . . ' He shook her gently. 'I wanted to punish you.'

'You did that,' she said. 'Every time you've looked at me since, I've wanted you to kiss me again.' She looked up at him expectantly.

'And yet I was afraid,' he admitted. 'I wanted so much more than just a physical reaction. But I was afraid you'd hate me.'

She shook her head.

'But despite my fear, ever since then, I've regretted that I didn't take you up on that challenge to share your bed. It drove me crazy to have you there, right under my eyes, in every stage of undress. I started to curse the night I'd made that vow not to touch you!'

'You too?' she said softly.

'The night I left—I just couldn't stand it any more. It had all gone wrong. We'd been building trust. You'd mellowed, and softened somehow, and I hoped you could find love again. Then Alison turned up. I came home that night to tell you what she'd said, to make a clean breast of it. But you wouldn't listen. I told myself that there was no hope you could ever feel anything but hate for me.'

Her hands skimmed over his shoulders and clasped at the back of his neck. 'No hope at all?' she whispered.

Ty smiled a little, but he still held her a fraction of an inch away from him.

'So many years wasted,' she whispered, 'because of Alison's vicious nature and my stupidity.'

'We'll have to make up for lost time.'

Brooke smiled, but it was abstracted. 'Until tonight, I thought she was still at the hotel. And I was sure you were staying with her.' She looked up, puzzled. 'Where have you been?'

'Your father, wise man that he was, added a couch and a shower to his office.'

'That was after he married Alison,' Brooke murmured.

'I'm not surprised. It functioned, but it was hardly comfortable. It didn't matter, though. I couldn't have slept, anyway. I kept thinking about you.'

She brushed a gentle hand over his cheek. 'Are you coming in?'

'Will Tara and Emily be shocked?'

'They're gone. You'll have only me to entertain you.'

There was a gleam in his eyes. 'I'll settle for that.' He kissed her, hard, and set her aside. 'I hope you have a key,' he said. 'I seem to have misplaced mine.'

'I'll have to find you one.' She paused inside the door, for just a second.

Mother? she thought. Dad? Am I doing the right thing?

It seemed to her the house itself answered, with a contented little sigh.

'Well,' said Ty, 'if that takes care of everything on this agenda . . . '

'All the old stuff, at any rate.' She turned to him with a smile. 'From now on, Ty, it's all new business.'

'Which reminds me,' he said. 'I've been thinking of some very interesting places to have our future stock-holders' meetings. How about Hawaii, next winter?'

Brooke looked innocently up at him. 'Must we wait so long for a honeymoon?'

He drew a deep breath, and pulled her into his arms again. It felt to Brooke as if she had always belonged there, and as she looked up into his eyes, she knew that the shadows which had haunted them were gone for ever.

BETTY NEELS'
75th ROMANCE

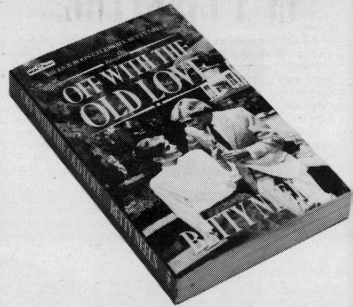

"OFF WITH THE OLD LOVE"

Betty Neels has been delighting readers for the last 17 years with her romances. This 75th anniversary title is our tribute to a highly successful and outstandingly popular author.

'Off with the Old Love' is a love triangle set amongst the rigours of hospital life, something Betty Neels knows all about, as a former staff nurse. Undoubtedly a romance to touch any woman's heart.

Price: £1.50   Available: July 1987

Available from Boots, Martins, John Menzies, W. H. Smith, Woolworths, and other paperback stockists.

FINDING LOVE TWICE IN A LIFETIME.

Scientific research and foreign agents force a girl to assume a new identity. Her past is all but wiped out.

At a chance meeting in a skiing chalet, Amanda finds herself strangely attracted to Craig. He in turn is reminded of a woman he once loved.

Amanda's Victorian seafront house in Seattle, and the memories of a Florida beach finally provide the missing pieces to a puzzling jigsaw of love and intrigue.

A powerful new novel from Rebecca Flanders.

Price: £2.25 Available: July 1987 W⬤RLDWIDE

Available from Boots, Martins, John Menzies, W. H. Smith, Woolworths, and other paperback stockists.

A TALE OF ILLICIT LOVE

'Defy the Eagle' is a stirring romance set in
Roman Britain at the time of Boadicea's rebellion.
Caddaric is an Iceni warrior loyal to his Queen. The lovely
Jilana is a daughter of Rome and his sworn enemy.
Will their passion survive the hatred of war,
or is the cost too great?
A powerful new novel from Lynn Bartlett.

W●RLDWIDE

Price: £3.50   Available: August 1987

Available from Boots, Martins, John Menzies, W.H. Smith,
Woolworths and other paperback stockists.